A Novelization by Todd Strasser
Based on a Screenplay by Jonathan Hensleigh and Greg Taylor & Jim Strain
Based on a Screen Story by Greg Taylor & Jim Strain and Chris Van Allsburg
Based on the Book by Chris Van Allsburg

Scholastic Inc.

New York Toronto London Auckland Sydney

TO JOSH BURACK, WHO HUNG TOUGH

No part of this publication may be reproduced in whole or in part, or stored in a retrieval system, or transmitted in any form or by any means, electronic, mechanical, photocopying, recording, or otherwise, without written permission of the publisher. For information regarding permission, write to Scholastic Inc., 555 Broadway, New York, NY 10012.

ISBN 0-590-67910-4

12 11 10 9 8 7 6 5 4 3 2   5 6 7 8 9/9 0/0

Printed in the U.S.A.   40

First Scholastic printing, December 1995

PROLOGUE

BRANTFORD, NEW HAMPSHIRE 1869

Deep in the New England forest the howling wind bent the trees back, rattling their limbs and snapping off great branches as if they were twigs. The harsh rain ripped through the dark air at a wind-blown angle, and the forest creatures cowered in their dens.

Crack! Lightning tore a bright gash in the stormy night sky and thunder rumbled ominously. At the side of a narrow muddy road a pair of horses hitched to a small wooden wagon whinnied in fear and stamped the ground with their hooves.

A dozen yards away, in the dark shadows beneath the shaking trees, two young brothers bent over in a deep hole, digging furiously. Their pants were muddy and their faces streaked with dirt and rainwater. Their shovels scraped and clanked as they pitched clod after clod of earth out of the hole.

"Deep enough!" yelled the older boy in a voice filled with fear and urgency.

He and his younger brother flung their shovels to the side and they scrambled out of the hole. Together they started toward the wagon, but fear stopped the younger boy a dozen feet away. The older boy reached into the back of the wagon and started to slide an iron lockbox out of it.

The box was heavy and the older boy couldn't handle it alone. "Come on!" he yelled at his younger brother. "We're almost rid of it!"

Pale with fear, the younger boy came forward to help his brother drag the box into the woods. At the edge of the hole they grunted and pitched the box in.

"*Help!*" Suddenly the younger boy lost his footing on the muddy ground and tumbled into the hole, falling on top of the box.

Brummm-tum-tum Brummm-tum-tum . . . a mysterious, but all too familiar drumming sound rose up out of the hole.

"*It's after me!*" the younger boy screamed in terror and frantically pawed the dirt at the side of the hole, desperately trying to escape. But his feet kept slipping back, as if whatever was inside the box was trying to keep him down in that gravelike cavity.

"Grab on!" his older brother shouted, leaning over the edge and reaching down. The younger boy stretched up, grabbed his brother's slippery hands, and felt himself get pulled out.

Brummm-tum-tum! Brummm-tum-tum! As if angered, the drumming in the box grew louder.

"*Run! Run!*" the younger boy cried hysterically and started away.

"No!" His older brother grabbed him by the shirt and pulled him back. "We have to finish this! Come on! Help me bury it!"

The older boy grabbed his shovel and began to pitch the loose earth back into the hole. His younger brother joined him. The drumming sound began to fade as the box disappeared under the dark, wet soil.

Boom! Thunder crashed and lightning crackled above as the exhausted boys dragged their shovels back to the wagon and climbed in. The older boy cracked a whip, and the horses were all too eager to go.

With his wet hair plastered to his head and his teeth chattering, the younger boy looked back at the spot where they'd buried the mysterious box.

"What if someone digs it up?" he asked with a shiver.

"May God have mercy on his soul," replied his brother. He yanked on the reins and they rode away through the dark, stormy night, never to return.

BRANTFORD, NEW HAMPSHIRE 1969

It was a warm September afternoon. A slight, thin twelve-year-old boy pedaled his new three-speed English racer down the tree-lined main street of town, past the low brick and clapboard buildings. As he passed the bakery, the florist, and a clothing store, he waved to the merchants and pedestrians, all of whom waved back.

After all, the boy's name was Alan Parrish and his family was the richest in town.

Alan continued to pedal. He was a friendly young man and not at all affected by his family's wealth. Even as he rode through the town square and passed the tall bronze statue of his great-great-grandfather Angus Parrish, a Civil War hero, he had other thoughts on his mind.

"Prepare to die, Parrish!" The sound of Billy

Jessup's voice sent a chill through Alan. Twisting around, he saw Billy and a group of boys with long hair racing toward him on bikes. Alan instantly leaned into the pedals of the English racer and started to pump as if his life depended on it.

"Hey, Parrish!" Billy yelled with a cruel laugh as he and his friends sped after him. "What's the rush?"

Alan pedaled furiously. It was easy to laugh when it was five against one. As long as you weren't the one! He turned onto a street lined with tall old oak trees. Alan kept riding as hard as he could, but glancing over his shoulder he could see the boys behind him catching up, with Billy Jessup in the lead.

"Come on, Parrish!" Billy yelled gleefully. "Let's get it over with!"

Ahead was a parking lot, and just beyond that a tall brick building. A large sign on the side of the building read:

PARRISH SHOES—FOUR GENERATIONS OF QUALITY

Alan raced through the gates of the parking lot, then jumped off his bike and ran into the building. Behind him, Billy and the other boys skidded to a stop.

"Go ahead, Parrish!" Billy yelled. "Run to Daddy! Just remember, we'll be waiting!"

In the cool shadows just inside the factory doors, Alan paused to catch his breath. He'd escaped . . . *for now.* Alan composed himself and started up the steps. The strong, sharp smell of new leather greeted him.

He reached the top of the stairs. A cavernous factory as big as a football field stretched out before him, filled with the echoing din of machinery and workmen's voices. Alan started down a long aisle lined with men cutting patterns out of leather and sewing shoe parts together.

Thunk-a-thunk-a-thunk! He paused beside the loud, rumbling sole-stamping machine that chopped shoe soles out of the leather. Carl Bentley, a twenty-year-old man, looked up and smiled.

"Hey, my man, Alan!" he said.

Relieved to hear a friendly voice, Alan turned toward him. "Hi, Carl."

"Let me show you something," Carl said, pausing from his work on the assembly line to reach into a drawer. "I've been working on this for almost a year now. I've got an appointment to show it to your father this afternoon."

Carl pulled a shoe out of the drawer. Alan had never seen anything like it before. It was some kind of sneaker, made with canvas and white leather over a rubber sole.

"What do you think?" Carl asked eagerly, handing the sneaker to Alan.

"Uh, what is it?" Alan said uncertainly.

Carl's jaw dropped. "What is it? It's a prototype of the *future!* In a couple of years, there's gonna be a pair of these in every closet in America. This shoe is gonna be the height of fashion and . . ."

Alan didn't hear the rest. Still worried about Billy Jessup and his friends, he'd walked over to a window and was looking down at the parking lot.

"Something wrong?" Carl asked, joining him.

"Uh, no, nothing." Alan never talked about his problems.

The familiar smell of pipe smoke drifted toward him. Alan turned and saw his father walking along the assembly line. Sam Parrish was in his early forties. He had thinning brown hair, smoked a pipe, and wore a tie and jacket. He owned the shoe factory and never seemed to go anywhere without two or three assistants following him.

"What are you doing here?" Mr. Parrish sternly asked his son. "I've told you before, this factory isn't a playground."

Alan put Carl's prototype sneaker down on an idle conveyor belt. "I, er, wanted to see if you could give me a ride home."

Mr. Parrish narrowed his eyes. "Billy Jessup again?" he guessed.

Alan wasn't surprised his father had figured out

8

the real reason he'd come to the factory. He started to regret that he'd come there seeking refuge.

"I've told you this before, son," Mr. Parrish said. "You're going to have to deal with that bully sooner or later."

Alan wanted to explain that it wasn't just Billy, but four of his friends as well. But he was already feeling humiliated enough in front of Carl and the men who always followed his father around.

"If you're afraid of something, you've got to face it," Mr. Parrish said and gave Alan a pat on the shoulder. "Now, get along, son."

It was no use trying to explain. Alan shrugged and started back through the factory. Suddenly a horn began to blare behind him. Alan turned and saw men scurrying around, waving their arms and yelling. Something was wrong with the sole-stamping machine. Alan could feel the vibrations in the floor as it began to shudder and smoke. Bolts were flying and blades snapped.

Then all at once, it went dead. Silence descended on the factory floor as all the workers stopped what they were doing and looked at the machine. Alan watched his father pull open a latch on the side of the machine and yank out a gnarled handful of leather and canvas strips.

It was Carl's prototype! Alan realized with a start. Meanwhile, his father's face was red with anger.

"Who did this?" he demanded.

Carl Bentley swallowed nervously. Across the factory, Alan wanted to yell out that it wasn't Carl's fault, that *he'd* accidentally put the prototype on the conveyor belt. But he couldn't bring himself to suffer his father's scrutiny again.

Instead, he hurried down the steps and back out into the sunny parking lot. His bike was still there, and Billy and his pals seemed to have gone. Breathing a sigh of relief, Alan got on his bike and started to ride away.

But no sooner was he out of the parking lot than Billy and his friends appeared from behind the trees and blocked his path.

"Going somewhere?" Billy asked with a nasty grin.

Alan quickly looked around, but it was no use. He was surrounded.

Alan felt himself start to tremble, but fought it down. Billy Jessup stepped toward him.

"Just because you're a Parrish doesn't mean you can hang around with my girlfriend," Billy said.

Alan couldn't believe it. "You mean Sarah? But we've always been friends."

"Not anymore," Billy said, balling up his fists and moving toward him.

A second later, all five boys were on him, kicking and punching. Alan fought back, but he didn't have a chance.

It was over in less than three minutes. Laughing and jeering, Billy and his friends left, taking Alan's new English racer with them. Alan struggled to his feet. His head was throbbing and his lip was split. Blood from his nose and mouth had splattered all over his shirt, but it didn't matter because the shirt was ripped anyway.

Jerks, he thought as he started to trudge home along the tree-lined road. No way was he going to let his father see him in that condition.

Brummm-tum-tum Brummm-tum-tum . . . he hadn't gone far when a strange drumming sound reached his ears. Alan looked around, but saw nothing that the sound could have come from. He shook his head, and started along the road again.

Brummm-tum-tum Brummm-tum-tum . . . there it was again. Alan put his fingers in his ears, wondering if Billy had given him a concussion.

Brummm-tum-tum! Brummm-tum-tum! The drumming only grew louder. Alan felt as if it was calling him. Curious and puzzled, he started to follow the sound.

The sound led him to a construction site. A sign said: "Future Executive Offices of Parrish Shoes." But all Alan saw were a big yellow bulldozer and backhoes digging huge gaping holes in the ground.

Brummm-tum-tum! Brummm-tum-tum! Alan followed the drumming sound. All around him construction workers wearing hard hats went about their work as if they didn't hear a thing. Were they deaf?

A truck horn blared and the workers put down their tools. Alan saw a silver snack truck parked at the edge of the construction site. It must have been time for a coffee break. Everyone left the site and headed for the truck. Except Alan, who was still following the sound of the drums.

Finally, he found the hole it was coming from. Alan jumped down and stood there, surrounded by dirt walls.

Brummm-tum-tum! Brummm-tum-tum! It was coming from a spot in the dirt wall. Alan picked up a shovel and scraped away some dirt. A rusty, reddish brown handle appeared. Alan grabbed it and pulled.

Thump! The lockbox fell to the bottom of the hole. The drumming stopped and everything became quiet. Alan stared down at it. He'd never seen anything like it before. An ancient lock kept the box closed, but it was completely rusted.

Clang! Alan hit the lock with the shovel and it instantly fell off. Imagining that it was filled with ancient treasures, Alan bent down, and lifted the top of the box. *What the . . . ?* It was filled with sand. Nothing but sand.

Disappointed, Alan started to climb back out of the hole.

Brummm-tum-tum Brummm-tum-tum . . . the drumming started again. Alan felt goosebumps rise on his skin. He quickly turned back to the box and plunged his hands into the sand. They hit something hard, and he wrestled out a wooden box.

Alan stared down at it in wonder. It looked like

a chess or backgammon board. The fold-up kind with brass hinges and a clasp. And it was decorated with carvings of jungle animals, landscapes, and a great white hunter in a pith helmet. Above all that, in elaborate and fanciful type, was the word JUMANJI.

Alan had never heard of it, and wondered if it was some kind of game. He shook the box and things inside rattled. Intensely curious, he undid the clasp and opened it ever so slightly . . . just for a peek.

A flash of glorious, rich color seeped out. Alan was stunned.

"So I think we better start laying the foundation here."

"Ferro-concrete or cinder blocks?"

Alan heard the voices of men coming back to the site. He snapped the box shut and scampered out of the hole. Whatever this thing was, he was going to take it home and give it a closer look.

Various chores, and a long explanation to his mother about what had happened to his nose and clothes, kept Alan from opening the Jumanji box until later that evening. He sat alone at the long wooden table in the dining room. Hanging on the walls around him were portraits of the famous men and women of the Parrish family who'd sat at that table decades before. His great-great-grandfather's Civil War saber hung over the fireplace.

Slowly and carefully, he opened the box. It unfolded into a game board. From the edges of the board, four different paths curled and wound their way toward a strange cloudy grasslike circle in the center. In a small side compartment he found tokens and dice.

Alan picked up one of the tokens. It was carved like a miniature African totem.

"Hard work, determination, and a cheerful outlook . . ." His father's words drifted toward him from the large, marble-lined foyer. Alan quickly snapped the board closed and hid it under his chair.

"These attributes have exemplified the Brantford spirit since our forefathers first settled this town," his father was saying.

Alan relaxed a little as he realized his father was not delivering this latest lecture to *him*. Instead, he appeared to be practicing it for an audience he would face later that night.

"Despite the granite of our soil, and the harshness of our native climate, we have . . . we have . . . darn it, what?"

"Wasn't it prospered?" Alan heard his mother offer. "Or was it persisted?"

"I can't remember," his father said. "I had the whole thing memorized this morning, but I've forgotten."

"Well, darling," Alan heard his mother say. "If you can face the town council, you can certainly face your son."

Alan stiffened. *Oh-oh.* His father *did* have something to tell him.

A second later his father strode into the dining room wearing a tuxedo. His mother followed in a red and white evening gown. She was the first to speak.

"Alan, darling, I told your father what you told me this afternoon," she said. "That it wasn't just Billy Jessup."

"If I'd known there were five boys," Mr. Parrish said awkwardly, "I wouldn't have lectured you."

Wishing to spare his father any further embarrassment, Alan told him it was okay. He hoped his parents would go, but they lingered. His mother kept nodding at his father, as if there was something she wanted him to say.

"Well, er, I want you to know that I'm proud of you for facing them even though you were outnumbered," Mr. Parrish continued, fumbling for something in his pocket. "And since you took it like a man, I want you to see this."

He handed Alan a brochure with a photograph of some ivy-covered red brick buildings on the cover. It looked like a college campus.

"Your mother and I have decided that you're ready to go to the Cliffside Academy for Boys," his father said. "You proved it today."

"Congratulations, sweetheart," his mother chimed in.

Alan felt numb, as if he'd just gone into shock. The Cliffside Academy for Boys was a prep school in Connecticut.

17

What was happening was instantly obvious. His parents were getting rid of him.

"You don't want me living here anymore." The words spilled out of his lips.

"Oh, Alan, how could you possibly *think* such a thing?" his mother gasped.

"You're ashamed of me for getting beat up all the time," Alan said.

"Absolutely not," his father insisted. "I just told you how proud I am of you."

Sure, Alan thought.

"It's always been the plan that you'd go to Cliffside when you were ready," his father added. "We Parrish men have been going there since the seventeen-hundreds."

Feeling miserable, Alan pulled his glasses out of his pocket and studied the brochure more closely. He instantly wished he hadn't.

"Look at this," he said, pointing at one of the pictures. "'Parrish Hall.'"

"It's the main dormitory," his father explained.

"Great." Alan rolled his eyes. "I get beat up here because my name is Parrish. I can't wait to see what they'll do when I'm living in a building named after my family."

His father looked shocked. "It was named after my father."

All the frustration that had been building since the fight suddenly spilled out of Alan. "Good," he snapped bitterly. "Why don't *you* go and live in it?"

His father stiffened, holding back a more angry response. "I did live in it. And I wouldn't be who I am today if it weren't for my years there."

"So?" Alan asked angrily. At that moment he hated being a Parrish. All it meant to him was getting picked on and beat up.

His father clenched his jaw. "Don't get smart with me, son."

"I'm not," Alan shot back. "Maybe I don't want to be who you are! Maybe I don't even want to be a Parrish!"

His father's face turned red with anger. Mrs. Parrish put a hand on her husband's shoulder to calm him.

"Believe me, son," Mr. Parrish growled through clenched teeth. "You won't be, not until you start acting like one!"

"So I guess I'm not ready to go to Cliffside after all," Alan said, drawing the conclusion he'd hoped for.

"We're taking you there next Sunday," his father replied in an icy voice. "And I don't want to hear another word about it."

"You won't!" Alan almost yelled. "I'm never going to talk to you again!"

Father and son glared at each other. At that moment it seemed to Alan that it was all his father's fault. Alan hated, *hated* being a Parrish, he hated living in this house, and being next in line to inherit that dumb shoe company. He hated all of it!

Without another word, Mr. Parrish turned and signaled his wife to follow him out of the room. Alan sat silently and watched them go. As soon as his father pulled the door closed, he picked up the Cliffside brochure and tore it into little pieces.

Forget it! He wasn't going there. Ever! Alan jumped out of his seat and headed upstairs. He was leaving, getting out, going somewhere where no one had ever even *heard* the name Parrish.

4

A little while later, Alan carried a small suitcase toward the front door. Inside were some clothes, peanut butter, cookies, and that Jumanji game. He was just about to pull the front door open and storm out when *ding-dong!* the doorbell rang.

Now what? Alan quickly hid the suitcase under a table in the foyer and pulled open the door. Outside stood Sarah Whittle, a pretty blond thirteen-year-old, who, unfortunately, was the source of a great deal of Alan's misery. Behind her was Alan's English racer.

"Oh, it's you." Alan turned and picked up the suitcase.

"Going somewhere?" Sarah asked.

"Yeah, I'm . . ." He stopped. Maybe he

shouldn't tell her. "I was just going over to Billy's to get my bike." He stepped past her.

"With a suitcase?" Sarah asked suspiciously.

Alan didn't answer. Instead, he started to strap the suitcase to the book rack behind the bike seat. The truth was, he'd had a mad crush on Sarah since the age of ten. But the only thing it had gotten him was a black eye and a swollen lip.

"I told Billy that if he didn't give you your bike back I wouldn't go to the movies with him this weekend," Sarah said.

"Great, thanks a lot." Alan's words were heaped with jealous sarcasm.

"Hey, I just wanted him to stop picking on you," Sarah explained. "I was trying to do you a favor."

"Save it for your boyfriend." Alan snapped the kickstand up and started to push the bike away.

"Billy's *not* my boyfriend," Sarah replied. Then she added, "But at least he's my age."

That was the big problem. Alan was a year younger than she was.

"Yeah, but mentally I could be his grandfather," Alan said, continuing down the front walk with his bike. "And I'm only ten months younger than you."

"But you're so *immature*," Sarah said behind him.

"Fine," Alan shot back over his shoulder. "Have a great life with Billy."

Brummm-tum-tum Brummm-tum-tum . . . Alan

froze. The drumming sound had started in his suit-case. After a moment it stopped.

"What was that?" Sarah asked.

"Nothing." Alan started to push the bike again.

Brummm-tum-tum Brummm-tum-tum . . . it started again. Sarah came closer and stared at the suitcase.

"What's in there?" she asked, mystified.

Alan looked out at the road. He really wanted to get going, but he really wanted to show her the game too. Finally the game, and Sarah, won.

"You gotta see this," Alan said, turning the bike around and heading back toward the house. "It's really cool."

Moments later they went through the glass French doors between the living room and din-ing room. Alan put the suitcase on the floor and opened it.

Brummm-tum-tum! *Brummm-tum-tum!* The drumming grew louder as he took out the game board and opened it. Sarah watched, fasci-nated.

"It's so weird," Alan said. "I mean, where does the drumming come from?" He picked up the cover and read about the game. "'Jumanji. A game for those who seek to find a way to leave their world behind.' The first to get to the end of the path and yell 'Jumanji' wins."

Sarah picked up the dice and studied them dis-

23

dainfully. "I quit playing board games five years ago."

She dropped the dice onto the board. One rolled a 4, the other a 2. Suddenly one of the tokens moved to the sixth square. It seemed like magic. Sarah and Alan gaped at the board, then at each other.

"It must be magnetized or something," Alan said, picking up the dice.

But Sarah was hardly listening. Her eyes went wide as she pointed at the glasslike lens in the center of the board. Words were appearing in the glass . . . like it was some kind of crystal ball.

"'At night they fly, you better run,'" Alan read. "'These winged things are not much fun.'"

The letters faded away. Suddenly Alan heard flapping and fluttering sounds coming from the fireplace.

"What's that?" Sarah asked apprehensively.

"I don't know, maybe a bird or something," Alan said. But deep inside he knew it wasn't a bird. Something weird was going on. Weird and scary.

"Put it away," Sarah said, meaning the board.

"Yeah, you're right." Without thinking, Alan dropped the dice on the board. They rolled a 2 and a 3. Now another token moved to the fifth square.

"Uh—oh!" Alan gasped as more words began to appear in the crystal. "'In the jungle you must wait, until the dice read five or eight.' What's *that* mean?"

Suddenly Sarah shrieked, *"Alan, what's happening to you?"*

Alan didn't have a clue what she was talking about. "What do you mean? Nothing's happening . . ." Then he looked down at his body. His legs were turning into smoke! And the smoke was being drawn into the game board!

"Wha . . . *ahhhhhhhhhhh!*" A scream of terror ripped through Alan's throat as his whole body was transformed into smoke and was sucked into the board. The next thing he knew, he was looking up at Sarah and the living room and the chandelier hanging from the ceiling as if it was all through a fish-eye lens.

"Alan? *Alan!?*" Sarah was screaming down at the board. As Alan watched helplessly from inside she suddenly looked away. Another scream tore through her throat as hundreds of big black bats burst from the fireplace, swooping and diving at her.

In a flash she was up and gone. Alan was left behind, somewhere inside the game.

5

THE PRESENT

Eight-year-old Peter Shepherd was not happy. Ever since his parents were killed in that car crash in the Canadian Rockies, his life had been a jumbled, mixed-up mess. At the moment, Peter and his twelve-year-old sister Judy found themselves standing on the front lawn of a big, old, creepy-looking house in Brantford, New Hampshire.

They were with their Aunt Nora, a slightly uptight lady in her thirties who appeared to have taken over their lives now that their parents were gone. The problem was, Aunt Nora had never been married and had never had kids. She knew as much about having kids as a plumber knows about brain surgery.

"Judy! Peter!" Aunt Nora waved at them from the front door. "Come look at this."

Judy gave Peter a sullen look and they started toward the front door of the house. Aunt Nora was looking for a big house to buy so she could turn it into something called a bed and breakfast. When Judy asked what that was, Nora had said it was sort of a cross between an inn and a private home. Peter still wasn't sure what she meant by that.

He and his sister stepped into the house and looked around. They were standing in a room with a marble floor. A chandelier made of a zillion pieces of glass hung from the ceiling. The house smelled old and musty. Peter walked into the living room. All the furniture was covered with old yellowed bedsheets and there were dust and spiderwebs everywhere. Peter couldn't imagine why anyone would want to stay there.

Aunt Nora was walking around with another lady, who was older than she was and had long bright-red fingernails.

"I'm going to put a reception area right here," Aunt Nora told the lady. "And a bar over there in the parlor."

"That sounds lovely," the red-nail lady said. Peter had noticed that no matter what Aunt Nora said, the red-nail lady said it sounded lovely.

Now the red-nail lady looked down at Peter. "So, what do you think, young man? Is this place big enough for you?"

Peter turned and walked out of the room.

Behind him he heard Aunt Nora tell the red-nail lady that he hadn't said a word since the accident. The red-nail lady pretended to be sad and said it was awful. That got Peter's sister Judy started.

"It's okay," she told the red-nail lady. "We barely knew our parents. They were always away skiing or gambling and sailing. We didn't even know if they loved us, but when their boat started to sink they wrote us a really beautiful good-bye note which someone found in a champagne bottle."

It was all a lie, but that was the only way Judy seemed to be able to deal with her parents' death. Aunt Nora took the red-nail lady aside and whispered something.

After a while the red-nail lady left and Aunt Nora made them help her unpack the car and bring in the boxes and suitcases. Then she took them out for pizza and ice cream. When they got back, it was time to go to bed.

Peter went into his new bedroom and Judy went into hers. Aunt Nora came and said some dumb stuff about not being his mother, but how she was going to try her best anyway. It was the same thing she said almost every night. Then she left and Peter lay there and waited until he was fairly certain she wouldn't come back. Then he pulled open the drawer of the night table beside his bed and took out a photograph of his mom and dad.

Brummm-tum-tum Brummm-tum-tum . . . the

faint sound of jungle drums seemed to be coming from the ceiling.

Peter glanced up at the ceiling, then looked back at the photograph.

The doorknob began to turn. Peter had just enough time to slip the photograph back in the drawer before the door opened and Judy came in wearing pajamas with pink flowers on them.

"Move over," she said.

Peter slid over and made room in the bed, then Judy got in.

"Did you hear something before?" she asked.

Peter stared up at the ceiling and thought of the drums, but decided not to mention it.

"Me, neither," Judy said with a shrug, but Peter knew she was lying. He turned and faced her.

"I miss Mom and Dad," he whispered. "Do you?"

"No," Judy whispered back.

Peter studied his sister's face for a moment. "If you don't quit lying, you're gonna get sent to a shrink."

"Where do you think they're going to send *you* if you don't start talking?" his sister asked.

Peter didn't know the answer, and didn't want to talk about it. He turned over on his side and closed his eyes.

Brummm-tum-tum Brummm-tum-tum . . . the faint sound of drums began to beat again.

Peter's eyes snapped open. He glanced at his sister, who looked wide-eyed back at him. She snuggled closer and he pulled the blanket up tightly under his chin. It would be a long time before either of them fell asleep that night.

The next day at their new school, Peter and Judy learned all about the history of the house they'd moved into. At recess the other kids told them how twelve-year-old Alan Parrish vanished from the house twenty-six years earlier and was never seen again. Some kids said it was a kidnapping. Others said Alan's father chopped him up into little pieces and hid them all over the house.

Then Judy told the other kids how her parents were abducted by Maoist guerrillas in New Guinea where they'd gone to research some strange new rain forest viruses. Peter stood nearby and said nothing.

Then a big fat kid said Judy was lying. He said his mother was the red-nail lady who had sold the

Parrish house to their aunt, and that their parents had died in a car crash.

And that's when Peter went a little crazy and attacked the big fat kid. And the big fat kid just laughed and held him at arm's distance where Peter could swing all he wanted and not land a punch.

So Peter bit him as hard as he could on the arm and the big fat kid screamed and ran away. Then the other kids all surrounded Peter and called him an animal until Judy got through them and dragged Peter away.

"I can't believe I have to talk to the principal after just *one* day of school," Aunt Nora groaned that night in the kitchen where they were eating dinner. "What am I supposed to do with you? This is *not* my department."

"You better punish us," Judy suggested.

"What's the punishment for lying?" Aunt Nora asked, nervously twisting a napkin around her fingers. "Or for biting someone?"

"You should probably ground us," said Judy.

"Okay, you're both grounded," Aunt Nora said. Then she sighed. "Now . . . let's just try and relax and finish our dinner. Let's talk about something else."

A long silence followed. Then Judy cleared her throat.

"Well, we found out why no one else ever

bought this house," she said. Then she told Aunt Nora how twenty-six years before a kid named Alan Parrish had just disappeared and how everyone in town thought the house was haunted.

Aunt Nora's eyes started to grow wide and then slowly narrowed. "That's it!" she snapped. "I'm sick and tired of your lies, young lady. You're grounded!"

"You already did that one," Judy informed her.

Aunt Nora gave her a helpless look as if she didn't know any other good punishments.

"Send me to my room," Judy recommended.

Aunt Nora nodded wearily and Judy stood up.

"Just for your information," Peter's sister said. "That wasn't a lie."

Then she left the room. Peter and Aunt Nora finished dinner in silence.

The next morning Aunt Nora had to leave early. She gave Peter and Judy breakfast and made them sit on the stairs while she gave them instructions: "The school bus should be here any minute. There's a snack for you in the fridge when you get home. If I get held up at the permit office, I'll call."

Brummm-tum-tum Brummm-tum-tum . . . that was when the drums started banging faintly upstairs again. Peter and Judy looked up, then looked at their aunt, who just kept on talking as if she hadn't heard a thing. Then they looked at each other, then up again.

"Hello?" Aunt Nora put her hands on her hips and looked annoyed. "Are either of you listening to me?"

"Huh?" Judy frowned. The drumming stopped.

Aunt Nora sighed. "Maybe I should wait here with you until the bus comes. Did your parents used to put you on the bus?"

Peter started to nod, but Judy quickly shook her head and said, "No."

"Are you sure?" Aunt Nora asked.

"Positive," said Judy. "You can go. We'll be fine."

"All right, be good." Aunt Nora turned and went out the front door. Judy quickly got up and closed the door behind her. Then she turned to Peter.

"You *do* hear it," she said.

"Hear what?" Peter asked innocently.

Brummm-tum-tum Brummm-tum-tum . . . the drumming started again. It was clearly coming from above them. In a flash, they were both heading up the stairs to the second floor.

But on the second floor, the drumming was still coming from above. Judy looked nervously at the spiral staircase that led to the attic, then started up it. Peter followed.

But once they reached the attic, the drumming stopped again. Peter and Judy looked around, bewildered. The attic was filled with old furniture, paintings, sports equipment, and toys. There was even a piano, but no drums.

"Where was it coming from?" Judy asked in a low voice.

Peter shook his head. He didn't know. They split up and started to search.

Brummm-tum-tum! Brummm-tum-tum! Without warning the drumming started again right behind Judy.

"*Ahhh!*" Judy let out a scream and wheeled around.

Meanwhile, Peter ran over and began to dig through a pile of old plastic toys, jigsaw puzzles, and hockey sticks. At the bottom of the pile was a wooden box with the word JUMANJI carved in it.

Brummm-tum-tum! Brummm-tum-tum! The drumming was louder than ever and it was coming from the box.

Peter reached down to pick up the box. Just as he was about to touch it, the drumming stopped. He frowned at Judy, who nodded with encouragement. Peter picked up the box and set it gently on an old dresser. Then he carefully opened the clasp and unfolded the game.

"Wow!" Judy let out a deep breath as she studied the game board. Oddly, two tokens were already on it. Peter tried to move them, but they wouldn't budge.

"Weird," he said. "They're stuck."

From the side compartment he took out two more tokens and the dice. Meanwhile, Judy read the instructions on the cover.

Shuump! Suddenly the two loose tokens in Peter's hands were sucked onto their beginning squares on the board. Peter and his sister were shocked.

"It's gotta be microchips or something," Judy guessed.

Peter handed her the dice. "You go first."

Judy stared reluctantly at the dice in her hand. "Well, okay." She dropped the dice on the board.

Brummm-tum-tum! Brummm-tum-tum! The drumming started again, and Judy's piece moved by itself. She and Peter exchanged amazed looks. Then words began to appear in the crystal in the middle of the board.

"'A tiny bite can make you itch,'" Judy read. "'Make you sneeze, make you twitch.'"

A loud, buzzing sound reached their ears. Judy and Peter spun around just in time to see three mosquitos the size of sparrows zeroing in on them.

7

Peter had never seen mosquitos so huge. Judy quickly grabbed an old tennis racket and swung it.

Whack! She hit the lead mosquito. *Crash!* It smashed through an attic window. The other two mosquitos banked sharply and followed it outside.

Peter and Judy stared at each other in amazement, then looked down at the board. Peter picked up the dice, but Judy grabbed his hand.

"Don't!" she cried.

It was too late. Peter dropped the dice and rolled snake eyes.

Brummm-tum-tum! Brummm-tum-tum! The drumming started again. Peter actually hadn't noticed that it had stopped. New words began to appear in the crystal: "'This will not be an easy mission. Monkeys slow the expedition.'"

Crash! Clang! Thwack! A cacophony of loud breaking noises started to come from downstairs. Judy jumped up and raced toward the attic stairs. Peter picked up the dice and followed.

As they ran down the stairs toward the kitchen, they could hear the sounds of plates being smashed, and weird screeching cries. Judy stopped behind the kitchen door, then slowly pushed it open.

Inside a dozen large brown monkeys were tearing the kitchen apart. On one of the counters two monkeys threw porcelain cups at a third monkey who swung a ladle like a baseball bat, smashing them into dust. Other monkeys were throwing all the food out of the refrigerator, still others were throwing knives!

Judy quickly closed the kitchen door. She and Peter stared at each other, spellbound. Then Peter stared fearfully down at the dice in his hand. Without doubt, these were where all the trouble began.

"Listen, Peter," Judy gasped in a low urgent voice. "We better get back upstairs and look at that game."

In a flash they were racing back up the stairs. Gasping for breath, they burst back into the attic. Judy picked up the board and quickly read through the instructions: "Okay, you roll the dice and move."

"We know that," Peter said.

"'Doubles gets another turn,'" his sister read. "'The first player to reach the end and yell "Jumanji" wins.'"

"That's it?" Peter asked.

"No, there's this." Judy read, "'Adventurers beware: do not begin unless you intend to finish. The exciting consequences of the game will vanish only when a player has reached Jumanji and called out its name.'"

Creak! Wham! Downstairs, the front door opened and slammed shut. Judy and Peter raced to an attic window and looked down just as the monkeys fanned out across the lawn below, dispersing in a dozen different directions.

"We have to stop them!" Peter dashed back to the game and started to fold it up.

"No, wait!" Judy stopped him. "The instructions say the only way we can make it all go away is if we finish the game. We better do it or Aunt Nora's gonna pitch a fit!"

Peter glanced nervously at the game. So far they'd been attacked by giant mosquitos and had unleashed a bunch of maniac monkeys who'd destroyed the kitchen and were now running around Brantford doing who knew what!

Judy could see that her brother was reluctant to continue playing. "Listen," she said, "we'll get through it quickly. Just keep rolling the dice. I mean, there's no *skill* involved."

Peter hesitated, then unfolded the board and held the dice out to his sister.

"No." She shook her head. "Snake eyes is doubles. You get another turn."

Peter rolled a 3 and a 5. As his token moved across the board without being touched, words appeared in the crystal: "'His fangs are sharp, he likes your taste. Your party better move posthaste.'"

"Posthaste?" Judy scowled. She'd never heard of that.

The sound of crashing piano notes startled them. Peter and his sister spun around and squinted into a dark corner of the attic where an old piano stood. A huge lion emerged from the shadows, fixing them with its eyes.

Peter and Judy started to back away. Peter's mouth was open, but his throat was so tight with fear that no sound escaped.

GRRROAARRRR! The lion let out a fearsome roar. Peter and Judy bolted toward the door and flew down the spiral stairs.

Thwaammp! Somehow the lion leaped the entire stairs and cut them off on the second floor.

"*Ahhhhhh!*" Peter and his sister let out a collective scream and raced down the second floor hall in the other direction. They skidded to a stop. Standing before them was a wild man! He had long, stringy brown hair and a bushy beard. His clothes were stitched together out of animal hides and on his head he wore a primitive-looking hat made out of a tortoise shell. His clothes glistened with raindrops, as if he'd just stepped out of a tropical rain forest.

He had a crazy look in his eyes, and a crude-looking knife in his hand.

Caught between the wild man and the lion, Peter and Judy looked up and down the hall. At one end was the ferocious lion.

At the other was a wildman with a knife.

And they were trapped in the middle!

8

GRRROAARRRR! The lion attacked!

Given the choice between that huge deadly beast and the wild man, the kids headed for the man. To their surprise, he let them run right past. The next thing Peter knew, Judy pushed him into a linen closet and pulled the door closed, leaving it just open enough for them to peek out.

Meanwhile, the lion launched himself at the wild man!

At the last possible second, the wild man leaped up and grabbed the hall chandelier.

The lion missed him and landed hard on the carpet runner. His momentum sent him sliding right into Aunt Nora's bedroom.

The wild man let go of the chandelier and

dropped back to the hall floor. *Wham!* He kicked Aunt Nora's door closed.

GRRROAARRRR! Inside the bedroom, the lion roared in anger.

Blam! He charged the bedroom door and smashed into it. Five long claws ripped through the door, but the lock held.

In the linen closet, Peter and Judy held their breath as the wild man turned away from the door and touched the hallway wall as if studying it. He started down the hall toward them. Terrified, Peter and Judy backed deeper into the linen closet and pulled the door shut.

But the doorknob turned and the door flew open. The wild man looked in at them.

"Ahhhhhh!" Peter and his sister screamed. But the wild man hardly seemed to hear them.

Wham! He slammed the linen closet door closed. Inside the dark closet, Peter and Judy heard his footsteps start away. Once again Judy pushed open the door just enough to see. The wild man was standing in the middle of the hall with a stunned look on his face.

A second later he whipped around and bounded toward another door. He pulled on it, but it must have been locked.

Bam! He kicked the door down and went in.

As curious as they were frightened, Peter and Judy slowly emerged from the linen closet and went to the doorway the wild man had just gone through. Inside was a boy's bedroom, with posters of baseball players on the walls and plastic car models on the shelves. The wild man was standing beside an old English racer, running his fingers along the dusty frame.

They watched as he opened a closet door and gazed at the boy's clothing hanging inside. Then he turned toward a dresser and picked up a curled, yellowed photograph. From a pouch at his waist, he took out a battered pair of glasses that were much too small for his head. Holding the glasses up to his eyes, he studied the photograph for a long time.

Then he slowly turned toward Peter and Judy, who were still standing in the doorway.

"Did someone roll a five or an eight?" he asked.

Peter nodded.

"Yes!" the wild man cried and bounded toward him. Peter turned to run, but before he could, the wild man scooped him up in his arms and started to dance around the room shouting with joy. Then he stopped.

Thunk! He dropped Peter and ran out of the room.

Peter got to his feet and gave Judy a puzzled look. A second later they ran out of the room and down the stairs to the first floor, where the wild man was dashing from room to room.

"Mom! Dad!" he shouted. "Where are you? It's me, Alan! I'm home!"

Peter and Judy gave each other an amazed look. Could it really be the boy who vanished?

"Excuse me," Judy said. "You're not Alan Parrish, are you?"

Alan Parrish, now thirty-eight years old, spun around. "Who are you?"

"I'm Judy and he's Peter," Judy said. "We live here now."

Alan stared at them with a strange smile as if he didn't understand.

"This house has been empty for years," Judy explained. "Everyone thought you were dead."

Alan just kept staring at them. Finally his lips began to move. "So . . . where are my parents?"

Judy glanced nervously at Peter. "We don't know."

The smile disappeared from Alan's face. He turned and ran through the foyer and out the front door.

Peter and Judy followed. Alan crossed the lawn and stepped into the street, looking all around.

Screeech! A shiny brand-new police car coming down the street jammed on its brakes. To avoid being hit, Alan leaped into the air and landed on the car's hood.

The police car slid to a stop and the cop inside

jumped out, shouting at Alan, "Get down off my car!"

Alan got down.

"Step up on the sidewalk," the cop ordered. But instead of following Alan onto the curb, the cop looked back at the hood of the car and, using the sleeve of his shirt, rubbed the spot where Alan had stood until it shined again.

Meanwhile, Alan was staring into the police car with a fascinated look on his face.

"Excuse me," the cop said.

"What year is it?" Alan asked.

"It's brand-new," replied the cop, obviously referring to his car.

"No," said Alan. "I meant, what *year* is it?"

The cop stared at Alan as if he were crazy.

"It's nineteen-ninety-five," Judy said, coming up behind them.

"You got some ID?" the cop asked Alan.

But Alan was mumbling to himself. "Ninety-five minus sixty-nine . . . twenty-six years?"

"Let me guess," said the cop, staring at the stitched-together skins Alan was wearing. "You left your wallet in your other pants. Okay, maybe you can tell me this. You from around here?"

"Yes," said Alan, "but I've been in Jumanji."

"Huh?" The cop scowled.

"It's in Indonesia," Judy quickly said. "He was in the Peace Corps."

Meanwhile, Alan was studying the name on the cop's uniform. "Carl Bentley?"

Officer Bentley turned to Judy. "Is this man related to you?"

"Yes, sir." Judy lied like a pro. "He's our uncle."

Just then Peter noticed that two of the monkeys from the game were trying to crawl into Officer Bentley's car. Officer Bentley didn't see them, but Alan must have because he let out a loud roar that sounded just like a lion. In a flash the monkeys disappeared around the car. Officer Bentley frowned and turned to Judy again.

"Is he okay upstairs?" he asked.

"He suffered a head injury a few months ago," Judy quickly explained. "You know how when you're on a train you're not supposed to stick anything out the window?"

Ka-boom! A sudden explosion made everyone jump. Peter spun around and stared at Officer Bentley's car. Smoke was rising up through a blackened hole in the roof. The monkeys had gotten inside and one must've fired Officer Bentley's riot gun! The other one turned the ignition key!

Screeech! The cop car took off, burning rubber down the street. Peter couldn't see anyone driving, but he could hear wild monkey laughter coming from inside.

"Stop!" Officer Bentley shouted and started to run down the street after his new patrol car. No sooner had he left than Alan started to walk in the other direction.

"Wait!" Judy gasped. "Where are you going?"

"To find my parents," Alan replied.

"But what about the game?" Judy asked. "It says we have to finish."

"Go ahead and finish!" the wildman yelled back over his shoulder and continued on his way.

9

Instead of finishing the game, Judy and Peter followed him. Alan appeared to know the way into town. Soon he was strolling down Main Street, past a string of pawn shops, liquor stores, and boarded-up buildings. Alan walked along, looking this way and that, with a shocked expression on his face, as if he couldn't believe what his town had turned into. Not knowing what to say, Peter and Judy followed silently.

Alan passed through the town and headed toward a big brick building with broken windows. On the side of the building, a large, rusty sign, faded and peppered with bullet holes, read:

PARRISH SHOES—FOUR GENERATIONS OF QUALITY

Judy and Peter went through the gates and entered the factory behind Alan. Inside, the building was full of ancient, rusted machines. Birds chirped and flew around in the rafters above, and water dripped from the ceiling, leaving puddles on the floor.

They watched Alan bend down and pick up an old shoe box, cradling it in his hands like a broken doll. "Where is everybody?" he asked in a bewildered voice. "There used to be hundreds of workers. My dad made shoes here . . . the best shoes in New England."

Suddenly he saw something upstairs—the silhouette of a man smoking a pipe in the doorway. Alan tore up the stairs as fast as he could. Peter and Judy hurried behind him and watched as he pushed open the door.

Inside, an old man reclined in a chair, smoking a pipe. Some blankets were lying amid the garbage on the floor, and a pot of water steamed over a small propane stove. It appeared to Judy and Peter as if the old man was a bum who lived here.

The old man looked startled by the sudden intrusion.

Alan looked crushed.

"I'm sorry," he muttered to the old man. "I thought you were someone else."

They watched as Alan turned to leave, then

stopped and looked back at the old man. "Do you know what happened to the shoe factory?"

"It folded," the old man replied, relighting his pipe and puffing on it. "Like everything else in this town."

"What about the Parrish family?" Alan asked.

"After their kid disappeared, they put everything they had into trying to find him," the old man said. "After a while Sam stopped coming to work. He just quit caring."

Alan winced.

"Some of us tried to keep the place going," the old man said, "but I guess we just didn't have the Parrish touch."

Alan seemed to shiver. It was a little chilly, especially for someone who'd been in a jungle for the past twenty-six years. The old man pointed at a pile of clothes lying on the floor.

"You better take something," he said.

Alan picked out a pair of olive-colored flared slacks. "Are the Parrishes still around?" he asked as he pulled the slacks on.

"Oh, yeah," the old man said with an ironic smile. "They're over on Adams Street."

Peter and Judy followed Alan out of the factory, down several tree-lined streets, to a cemetery. Suddenly Alan slowed down. His shoulders stooped and his head hung low as he started to read the gravestones. They watched as he dropped to his knees, then took off his tortoise shell hat and placed it on a gravestone.

"I bet that's his parents," Judy whispered to Peter as they stood nearby and watched.

Alan pressed his face into his hands and muttered something about wishing his family didn't exist.

"Our parents are dead, too," Judy said. "They were in the Middle East, negotiating peace, when—"

Before she could continue, Peter poked her in the ribs. He'd had enough of her crazy stories.

"Our dad was in advertising," he said.

Judy stared at him in wonder. Except for her, this was the first time Peter had spoken to another human being since the accident. Alan stared at Peter, then got to his feet and started off through the graveyard.

"There he goes again," said Judy. "Come on."

They had to run to catch up to him.

"Listen," Judy said as she jogged alongside Alan. "I know you're upset and all, but I was hoping you could help my brother and me finish the game."

Alan shook his head. "Sorry."

"You could be a little grateful," Judy said. "Without us you'd still be stuck in there."

"I'm forever in your debt for getting me out," Alan replied, though not very sincerely. "But it wouldn't make a whole lot of sense if the first thing

I did was go and get stuck in there again, would it? I'm not interested in playing that game. I have too much catching up to do."

"But you don't understand," Judy said. "There's a lion in my aunt's bedroom!"

"Call a zoo," Alan replied tersely. "I'm out of the lion business."

Not knowing what else to do, they followed Alan out of the graveyard. The sound of a siren got Peter's attention. An ambulance was racing down Main Street.

Screeech! Tires squealed as the ambulance veered to avoid a car weaving erratically in the other direction. The vehicles clipped each other and skidded to a stop not far from where Alan, Peter, and Judy stood.

A paramedic in a white shirt and dark slacks jumped out of the ambulance and ran over to the car. He yanked open the door and pulled out the driver. Peter's jaw dropped. It was the red-nail lady! She was staggering and barely seemed conscious. Her skin was yellow and jaundiced, and her face glistened with sweat.

"Here's another one!" the paramedic shouted to his partner, who was pulling a stretcher out of the back of the ambulance.

"That's over fifty!" his partner yelled back. "What in the world's going on?"

Alan stepped closer and studied the red-nail lady's face. Then he cocked his head as if he was listening to something.

"Hear that?" he said to the kids.

"Hear what?" Judy replied. Peter didn't hear anything either, but it didn't matter. Alan heard something and it made him turn pale with fright.

"Quick! Move it!" he yelled, shoving them toward the red-nail lady's car. They piled into the front. Alan slid into the driver's seat and slammed the door closed.

"Think!" he urged them. "What came out of the game before?"

"There was the lion," Judy said. "A bunch of monkeys and—"

"That!" Peter cried, pointing through the windshield at a giant mosquito that had just landed on the hood. The mosquito peered through the windshield and poked it with its needlelike proboscis. Inside the car, the kids held their breath in fright.

"Don't worry," Alan reassured them. "He can't get us in here."

As if the mosquito had heard him, he flew off the hood and disappeared.

Ripppp! Something slashed through the car's convertible top. Looking up, Peter saw the mosquito's proboscis trying to reach them. He and Judy huddled as far away from it as they could.

Unable to reach them, the mosquito withdrew again.

"We're safe," Alan said with a sigh of relief. "Those things'll make you sick if they bite you, but if we go home and stay inside, we'll be okay."

Crack! They all looked up, startled. In a furious attempt to reach them, the mosquito had just smashed into the windshield, cracking it.

"How are we going to get home?" Judy asked.

Peter watched as Alan studied the car's dashboard. The keys were still in the ignition.

"Do either of you know how to drive?" Alan asked.

Judy and Peter shook their heads.

"I didn't think you looked old enough." Alan shrugged. "Okay, no problem." He reached for the keys. "My dad let me back the car down the driveway once and he used to let me sit in his lap and steer all the time."

He turned the key and the car started. "Okay, here we go!"

The engine revved as Alan pressed on the gas pedal, but they didn't move an inch. The lines in Alan's forehead deepened as he studied the dashboard again and started pushing and pulling buttons.

Peter heard a whirring sound as the convertible top started to retract.

"Alan!" Judy cried. "The top!"

Looking up, they saw the sky appear where the top had been. And growing larger and larger in the sky was the mosquito dive-bombing straight toward them!

Peter reached over and yanked on the thing he'd once seen his father yank on to make their car go.

Screeech! The car took off down the street, weaving and fishtailing as Alan tried to steer.

Crunch! Bang! Clang! Crack! In rapid succession they ran over a phone booth, a stop sign, fifty feet of picket fence, and a mailbox before finally coming to a stop in the front yard of the Parrish house.

Alan released a pent-up breath, grinned, and dusted his hands. "Piece of cake," he said cheerfully.

Meanwhile, Judy and Peter practically had to pry their hands off the dashboard and door handles. They'd even left fingermarks! Peter had been on some pretty scary roller coasters, but nothing that ever compared to this.

Alan pushed open the door and headed for the house. Judy and Peter followed, wondering what would happen next. It didn't take long to find out. When they got inside, Alan had disappeared!

They found him in the attic, standing in front of a mirror, holding an old wrinkled shirt up against himself. From an old trunk he pulled out a pair of pants.

"Alan?" Judy came up behind him with the Jumanji game. "When are you going to help us play?"

But at the sight of the game, Alan shrank back, his eyes wide with fear. "Keep that thing away from me!"

"But we have to finish before Aunt Nora comes home," Judy said pleadingly.

"Good, then I can inform her that she's the ex-owner of this house." Alan picked up a bundle of clothes and headed past them toward the attic stairs. "You realize that with my parents gone, this place is mine now."

They followed him down to the second floor, where he went into the bathroom and dropped the clothes. "How's the hot water these days? Did anyone replace that old boiler?"

Bang! He closed the door on Judy and Peter. Judy knocked. "You have to help us finish the game. What do you think those monkeys are going to do to the ecosystem around here? Hello?"

It was no use. The hissing sound of a running shower was Alan's answer. Peter gave his sister a quizzical look, as if asking, "What do we do now?" Judy answered by sitting down in the hallway outside the bathroom door. They'd wait.

When the bathroom door opened, a new man stepped out. He was wearing an old shirt and slacks, and his wet hair was much shorter, with a somewhat ragged look. His face was covered with red nicks and cuts that were blotted with little bits of toilet paper. The kids winced.

"Hey, what do you want?" Alan asked defensively. "I never shaved before."

They followed him down to the kitchen, which looked like a bomb had gone off in it. Tables and chairs were overturned, dishes and bowls smashed on the floor, and every surface covered with one sort of food or another.

Under the counter Alan found a bowl and, much to Peter and Judy's disgust, started to fill it with whatever half-decent morsels of food he could find.

"How about Peter and I play the game and you just sort of watch?" Judy asked.

"No, thanks." Alan shook his head. "I've seen all I want. Besides, I don't plan farther ahead than my next meal. I learned that the hard way." He held up a practically untouched donut. "Bingo!"

"Well, if you aren't going to help us, what are you going to do?" Judy asked.

Alan stopped and blinked as if he hadn't considered that before. "I guess I'll just pick up where I left off. I wonder if Mrs. Nedermeyer still teaches sixth grade?"

He reached for the refrigerator and pulled it open.

"*Ah!*" A small gasp of fright left his lips as a shivering monkey jumped out, screeched at him, and then ran out of the room. Peter watched as Alan took a moment to compose himself. It gave him an idea.

"Come on, Judy," he said, getting up. "Alan's not going to help us. He's afraid."

"What?" Alan spun around. "What did you say?"

"I said you're afraid," Peter replied. "But it's okay to be afraid."

"It's okay to be afraid," Alan repeated in a mocking tone. "I am *not* afraid."

"Prove it," Peter said.

Alan stared at him for a moment. "I don't have to prove anything to you."

Peter ignored him and turned to his sister. "Let's set the game up in the living room."

They started to leave the kitchen.

"Hey, listen," Alan said behind them. "You don't know what you're getting yourselves into."

"Whatever it is, we'll handle it ourselves," Peter replied. "We don't need you. Come on, Judy."

"You think monkeys and mosquitos and lions are bad?" Alan called after them. "That's kids' stuff. I've seen things that would give you nightmares for the rest of your life!"

Peter kept walking, pretending he wasn't impressed.

"I've seen things you can't even imagine!" Alan said behind them. "Snakes as long as a school bus, spiders the size of bulldogs, things that hunt in the jungle at night, things you don't even see. You just hear them running, and eating. You think it's okay to be afraid? You don't know what fear is. Believe me, you won't last five minutes without me."

That's when Peter stopped and turned. "So you're going to help us play?"

Alan must have realized that he'd backed himself into a corner. "All right! All right! I'll play!"

Peter breathed an immense sigh of relief. He noticed Judy staring at him in wonder.

"That was very cool," she whispered in awe.

"Reverse psychology," Peter replied. "Dad used to pull it on me all the time."

12

While Peter set the board up on the coffee table in the living room, Alan went around the room and pulled the shades closed.

"Everybody ready?" Judy asked, holding up the dice.

"Ready!" Peter said eagerly.

"Ready," Alan groaned reluctantly.

"Okay, here I go!" Judy tossed the dice. Everyone waited with bated breath.

Judy's piece didn't move. Nothing happened.

"I'll try again." Judy picked up the dice and rolled them.

Again, nothing happened. Peter and his sister looked over at Alan.

"It's not working," Judy said.

Alan rubbed his chin and stared at the board.

"No, right, of course not! It's not your turn!"

"It has to be," Judy said. "I rolled first. Then Peter went twice because he got doubles. Now it's my turn again."

"No, look." Alan pointed at the board. Four tokens stood on different squares. "Those two are yours. This one's mine. There's one more."

"Whose is it?" Judy asked.

Alan stared at the board again as the realization came over him. "You're playing the game I started in nineteen-sixty-nine!"

"So whose turn is it?" Judy asked.

"The person I was playing with," Alan replied. Peter and Judy waited for him to explain more, but Alan just gazed off into the air.

"Well," Judy finally said impatiently. "Who was it?"

"Sarah Whittle," Alan said.

"Who?"

Without a word, Alan stood up and left the room. Judy looked over at Peter.

"Here we go again," she said with a moan.

Alan left the house and started down the road. A little while later Peter and Judy followed Alan through a gate and up a walk toward a house. Trees hung over the walk and the lawn was long, unruly, and filled with weeds. The house itself looked run-down. Shutters hung by one hinge and the paint was peeling.

"This place gives me the creeps," Peter whispered to his sister as he looked around.

They stopped at a sign on the porch. In hand-painted purple letters it said: MADAM SERENA, PSYCHIC READINGS. BY APPOINTMENT ONLY.

Alan's shoulders sagged with disappointment. "I knew she wouldn't still be here."

"Let's at least ask," Judy said. "Maybe Madam Serena will know where Sarah went."

While Judy knocked on the door, Alan looked around the porch. "We used to play right here on this porch. It seemed a lot bigger in those days."

A moment later a muffled female voice came from the other side of the door. "Yes?"

"Can you help us?" Judy asked.

"Do you have an appointment?" the woman asked.

"No, we're just trying to find someone."

"Madam Serena can't see you right now," the woman said.

"Maybe you can help us," said Alan.

The door opened slowly and Peter saw a pretty lady with disheveled blond hair and puffy eyes. It looked like she'd been sleeping.

"We're looking for someone who used to live here," Alan explained.

The woman frowned and studied him closely. "I've lived here all my life."

"Then you must know Sarah Whittle!" Judy exclaimed.

"Why do you want Sarah Whittle?" the woman asked suspiciously.

For the last few seconds, Alan had been silently transfixed, staring at the woman. Now he said, "Sarah?"

"I . . . I don't go by that name anymore," the woman stammered, staring back at him.

"Sarah Whittle?" Alan said as if he could hardly believe it.

"What do you want?" the woman asked, narrowing her eyes at him.

"When you were thirteen, you played a game with a kid down the street," Alan said, stepping closer. "A game with drums."

Sarah blanched. "How do you know *that*?"

"Because I was there," Alan said.

She stared up at him, bug-eyed. "Alan?"

"Yes." Alan nodded.

Thunk! Sarah Whittle went stiff as a board and fell backwards in a dead faint.

13

They revived her and, with a great deal of persuasion, convinced her to come with them back to the Parrish house. There, while sitting in the living room on a couch, she insisted on making a phone call.

"Sounds like I got his answering machine," she muttered while the others tried not to listen. Peter heard a faint beep and then Sarah started to talk into the phone. "Dr. Boorstein, it's Sarah Whittle calling. I might need to have my dosage checked. You know the event we've been talking about for the past two decades? The one that didn't really happen? Well, I seem to be having another episode involving that little boy who didn't really disappear. I'm sitting in his living room drinking lemonade. I'd be very interested in your interpretation. Please call me at your next opportunity."

She hung up. "He'll call back at ten minutes to the hour."

Alan and the kids traded glances. "Okay, now while we wait . . . " He pulled the Jumanji board out from under the coffee table.

"*Ahhhhh!*" Sarah jumped to her feet. "Get that thing *away* from me!"

"You have to help us finish the game, Sarah," Judy said.

"No, I don't!" Sarah cried. "I've spent over two thousand hours in therapy convincing myself that thing doesn't exist! I made it all up about you turning into smoke and disappearing into the game because whatever *really* happened was just too awful!"

Alan nodded. "It was awful, but it was also real."

"No!" Sarah took a step back, still shaking her head.

"Listen," Alan said in a calming voice. "Twenty-six years ago we started something and now we're all going to finish it. And guess what?"

Sarah gave him an extremely apprehensive look as he took her hand . . . and dropped the dice in it.

"It's *your* turn," Alan said.

"I won't play." Sarah kept shaking her head.

"You *will* play," Alan insisted.

68

Sarah narrowed her eyes and hissed, "Just try and make me."

They glared at each other. Finally, Alan sat down. "All right," he said in a disgusted tone, holding out his hand. "Just give me the dice and get out!"

Sarah let go of the dice. Instead of catching them, Alan let them fall on the game board!

"How could you do that!" Sarah screeched. "That's not fair!"

"Sorry." Alan shrugged. "Law of the jungle."

Brummm-tum-tum! Brummm-tum-tum! The drumming started. Everyone stared at the board. Sarah's token slid itself forward. Meanwhile, Sarah stared daggers at Alan.

"When I think of all the energy I've put into visualizing you as a radiant spirit," she grumbled.

Words began to float up into the crystal, but Sarah refused to look at them.

"Go on," Judy urged her. "Read it."

But Sarah's eyes were locked on Alan. "Twenty-two years of Dr. Boorstein down the drain. All I can say is . . . I'm incredibly lucky I had health insurance."

"*Read it!*" Alan snarled.

Sarah took a deep breath and swallowed. "'They grow much faster than bamboo. Take care or they'll come after you.'"

Bits of plaster started to fall on the game board.

Everyone looked up at the ceiling where the green tendril of a vine forced its way through a crack in the plaster.

"Don't let this be happening!" Sarah moaned.

Peter looked around the room. Small vines had started to push out from behind pictures, from between sofa cushions, and out of the electrical sockets. Everyone backed into the center of the room.

"Stay away from the walls," Alan cautioned them.

The green tendrils began to bloom with purple flowers the size of sunflowers.

"Wow, they're beautiful." Sarah reached out to touch one, but Alan quickly grabbed her hand and pulled her back.

"Don't touch them!" he warned. "They shoot poison barbs. And don't get anywhere near the big yellow ones."

Judy looked around. "What big yellow ones?"

Suddenly Peter felt something curl around his ankle and tighten. "Help!" he cried, but it was too late. The vine yanked him off his feet and started to pull him under the rug.

"Get him!" Alan shouted.

They raced after him, but the vine was pulling too fast. Peter twisted around just in time to see a giant yellow pod appear at the far end of the room. The thing must have been four feet wide! Suddenly it opened, revealing yellow petals and pointed sharklike teeth.

It was a yellow one! And it was pulling him toward its gaping vegetable jaws.

"Noooooooooo!" Peter screamed in total terror.

At the last second, Alan dove forward and grabbed Peter's free ankle. Sarah and Judy each grabbed one of his hands. Then all three began to pull. They got into a tug-of-war with the vine, using Peter as the rope!

Grunting, straining every muscle, they pulled as hard as they could. Peter felt like his arms and legs were going to pop right out of their sockets.

And still the vine was pulling him closer to the huge yellow flower's teeth!

14

Frozen with terror and stretched to the limit, Peter's eyes stayed locked on Alan as the older man looked around desperately for something to use. Suddenly he lunged for the old Civil War saber hanging over the stone fireplace.

But in doing so, he let go of Peter!

"Heeeellllllppppp!" Peter screamed as the vine dragged him toward the yellow pod. His feet were only inches away!

Whack! Alan slammed the saber down, slicing the vine in two. Like a tug-of-war team whose rope accidentally breaks, everyone rocketed backwards and landed on the floor. Peter opened his eyes and saw a cloud of feathery white things floating in the air above him.

"Seeds," Alan said, getting to his feet. "Whatever

you do, *don't* open any windows. You wouldn't believe how fast these things grow."

He ran to the pair of French doors that separated the living room from the parlor and slammed them shut. New tendrils from the vine snaked up the other side of the glass, but they were unable to get through.

Meanwhile, Sarah was quietly backing toward the front foyer as if to escape. Just as she turned to run, Alan dashed across the room and grabbed her.

"Get your hands off me!" Sarah tried to twist out of his grasp.

"The game's not over yet," Alan grunted through clenched teeth as he struggled with her.

"It is for me!" Sarah kept fighting. "Let me go!"

But Alan dragged her back to the living room. Peter and Judy followed them and watched as Alan made Sarah sit down at the game board.

"We'll finish the game right here," Alan announced.

"This is so abusive," Sarah complained with a pout.

Judy picked up the dice and handed them to Alan. "It's your turn."

Sarah groaned again and shook her head. "The last time I played this game, it ruined my life."

"It ruined *your* life?" Alan's eyes went wide and manic. "What about *mine*? 'In the jungle you must wait, until the dice read five or eight.' Remember?

But they didn't read five or eight for twenty-six years *because somebody stopped playing!*"

Sarah winced sheepishly. "I . . . I was just a kid. I couldn't handle it."

She glanced at Peter and Judy, as if asking for their support.

"It's okay," Judy said. "We're scared too. But if we finish the game it's all supposed to go away."

"How do you know?" Sarah asked nervously. "How do you know it won't all happen again? How do *I* know I won't get stuck in the jungle next?"

Alan leveled his gaze at her. "Because, unlike some people, Sarah, I won't abandon my friends."

"Neither will I," said Judy.

Everyone looked at Peter, who put out his hand. Judy placed hers on top of it. And Alan rested his hand on top of hers, as if making a gesture of unity. They all turned to Sarah.

"Well?" Alan asked archly.

Sarah sighed and rolled her eyes, then reluctantly put her hand on top of the others. "I knew this was going to be a bad day."

"Relax," Alan said, shaking the dice in his hand. "All we have to do is roll with the punches and keep our heads. Everything's going to be fine."

With a smile brimming with reassurance, Alan dropped his dice. His token moved and new words began to float up into the crystal lens.

"'A hunter from the darkest wild makes you feel just like a . . .'" Alan turned pale and didn't finish the sentence.

"Child?" Judy guessed.

Alan shrank into a childlike crouch. His eyes darted around. "Van Pelt," he whispered with fright.

Blam! A shotgun blast shattered the French doors to the living room. A cloud of feathery vine seeds wafted toward them in the air.

"*Get down!*" Alan screamed, diving for the floor.

Peter dove, then looked back at the splintered French doors as a tall man with white hair and thick white mutton-chop sideburns stepped through them. He was wearing a khaki safari jacket and a large round pith helmet, and he carried a huge shotgun. The skin of his face was weathered and wrinkled and expressionless. His eyes scanned the room without blinking. This must have been the person Alan called Van Pelt.

Peter heard a rustle and was amazed to see Alan scurry away on his hands and knees, crawling frantically toward the doorway on the other end of the room. The tall white-haired man instantly raised the shotgun.

Blam! The shot made Peter's ears ring. Across the room the blast ripped a gaping hole in the edge of the doorway, showering Alan with splinters. Alan jumped up and ran.

"This isn't a foot race, lad!" Van Pelt shouted with a regal British accent. "Stand up straight and let me pop you fair and square!"

It was clear that Alan had other plans. The great white hunter pursed his lips and stepped through the living room. Peter and the girls cringed in terror, but Van Pelt showed no interest in them as he followed Alan's trail.

Blam! They heard another shot in the first floor hallway. Peter bit his lip. Had Alan been killed?

"Blast it!" Van Pelt shouted in frustration. "You're a disgrace to the species!"

Peter heard the front door creak loudly. Alan must have escaped! Peter jumped up and headed toward the front hall.

"Where are you going?" Judy yelled.

Peter didn't have time to answer. He had to see what happened next. He got to the doorway in time to see Alan race to the street. The police car was just pulling up as Alan shot past it. The car looked like it had suffered a lot of wear and tear since Peter had last seen it. Not only was there a big hole in the roof, but it was dented and scratched everywhere.

A second later Officer Bentley jumped out of the car. "Hey, you!" he shouted at Alan.

Blam! The shotgun went off, disintegrating the

limb of a tree just over Alan's head. At the sound of the blast, Officer Bentley spun around, crouched behind his cruiser, and drew his revolver.

"Drop that gun!" he shouted at Van Pelt. "Get your hands in the air!"

Blam! The great white hunter responded by blasting the patrol car. Officer Bentley instantly ducked.

Blam! Blam! Blam! In rapid succession Van Pelt blew out the windshield, the back window, the headlights, and, for good measure, the streetlight above Officer Bentley's head, sending a shower of glass down on him.

Meanwhile, Alan was still racing down the street. Van Pelt drew a bead on him. It looked to Peter like he had a clean shot. Peter shut his eyes, waiting for the blast.

Click! No blast. Peter opened his eyes and saw Van Pelt look down at his gun in disgust.

"Blast it all!" The great white hunter growled and then sprinted off through a hedge as if trying to find a shortcut to catch Alan. Peter could only assume he'd run out of ammunition.

For a moment there was quiet. Officer Bentley crawled out from behind the door and looked down at the remains of his brand-new patrol car, then jumped in and raced away, tires smoking as he squealed down the street.

Peter looked around and noticed that some of the vine seeds had floated out of the house and were drifting off in the breeze. He felt his shoulders sag. Alan was running for his life. They'd never get to finish the game. It was hopeless.

15

Completely dejected, Peter, Judy, and Sarah trudged back into the house and toward the living room.

"Something tells me that hunter guy has been looking for Alan for a long time," Judy said as they crossed the foyer.

"You're right," said Sarah. "And even if Alan gets out of *this* situation, the same thing is going to keep happening to him over and over."

Peter gave her a curious look, as if wondering how she could be so sure.

"When you carry so much repressed anger, it attracts a lot of negative energy," Sarah explained. "Alan didn't end up in the jungle by accident. There *are* no accidents."

They stepped into the living room. The walls

were covered with vines and purple flowers.

"Whose turn is it?" someone asked. Peter and the girls jumped around, startled to see Alan climbing in the living room window. He gave Sarah a wry smile.

"I go next," Judy said.

Meanwhile, Sarah glowered at Alan. "You might have warned us that there was someone in there with a gun trying to kill us."

"Is that hunter the reason you didn't want to play?" Judy asked Alan innocently.

"He didn't want to play either?" Sarah gasped and pointed a haughty finger at Alan. "Well, well, well, Mr. We-Started-Something-And-Now-We're-Gonna-Finish-It. The truth comes out."

"Why's he trying to kill you?" Peter asked.

"He's a hunter," Alan replied simply. "Right now he happens to be hunting me."

"But why?" Judy asked.

"I really don't know," Alan said with a sad shrug. "He seems to find everything about me so . . . offensive. You'd think he wouldn't want to waste his time."

"Have you ever tried sitting down and working out your differences?" Sarah asked.

"Are you *crazy*?" Alan asked. "You can't talk to him. He's—"

"Don't you *dare* call me crazy!" Sarah suddenly screamed. "Everyone thinks I'm crazy. Ever since I told the cops twenty-six years ago that you disappeared inside a board game."

"I wasn't calling you crazy," Alan said apologetically. "It was just a figure of speech."

"Maybe I should roll," Judy said impatiently, trying to get their attention. But Alan and Sarah ignored her.

"You know what it's like to be known as the little girl who saw Alan Parrish murdered?" Sarah asked emotionally. "You think anyone came to my fourteenth birthday?"

"Not even Billy Jessup?" Alan asked. "It sounds like his kind of scene."

"Billy who?" Sarah frowned as if she didn't know who Alan was referring to.

"Oh, come off it, Madam Serena," Alan scoffed. "I'm sure if you dig around in the lower reaches of your higher consciousness, you ought to be able to dredge up the memory of your boyfriend Billy. You were the perfect match. His anger wasn't repressed."

Peter had heard enough of this junk. He turned to his sister. "Go ahead, roll."

Judy rolled and her token advanced. A new rhyme floated up into the crystal lens: "'Don't be fooled, it isn't thunder. Staying put would be a blunder.'"

Peter and his sister shared a puzzled look. Meanwhile, Alan and Sarah were *still* bickering.

"Are you talking about that kid who used to take your bicycle?" Sarah asked.

"I'm talking about the guy you went to the movies with when you should have been finishing the game we started," Alan shot back.

The floor began to vibrate slightly. Peter could feel it. It felt like a train was coming toward them, but still very far away.

Oblivious to everything else, Sarah and Alan kept arguing.

"You were always so immature," Sarah said. "You're *still* immature!"

"I'm immature? At least I—" Alan suddenly stopped. "You hear that?"

Now Peter could hear the distant sound of rumbling that went with those vibrations. Alan walked over to the wall and put his hand on it. For a moment, everyone held their breath and was perfectly still. The vibrations seemed to be growing stronger and the rumbling was definitely growing louder.

Alan spun around. "Stampede!"

He dove toward Peter and the girls, driving them away from the wall.

Crash! Over his shoulder, Peter saw something more mind-boggling than anything he'd seen yet! The long, pointed horn of a rhinoceros smashed through the wall . . . followed a split second later by a huge rhino crashing through the wall as though it were paper.

"Run!" Alan cried as more rhinos crashed through. The air was filled with an unbelievable deafening din of hoofbeats and snorts.

Peter dove behind a couch, followed by the others as the herd of rhinos stampeded right through the living room.

Crash! They smashed headlong into the west wall of the house, creating a huge hole leading out to the lawn!

The thunder of pounding feet and wild trumpeting followed as a herd of rampaging elephants came next, followed by a racket of zebra hooves.

Moments later the only thing that remained was a cloud of dust and an eerie silence. From one end of the living room to the other was the path the animals had taken. Every object, table, lamp, and chair in the path had been pulverized. Peter and the others slowly rose from behind the couch to survey the damage. It looked as if a column of tanks had rumbled through.

Just when it seemed like nothing worse could happen, a flock of pelicans took them by surprise, gliding silently through the hole at the east end of the living room. The birds all passed right through except the last, a big feathery fellow who landed amidst the rubble near the game board.

The big bird cocked his head and eyed the board, then suddenly snatched it up in his bill and took off!

"Don't let him get away!" Alan cried.

The big bird flew back toward the hole in the east wall, but Alan and Judy blocked it, waving their arms excitedly. The pelican banked and headed toward the west wall and the open sky beyond it.

"Sarah! Peter!" Alan yelled. "Stop him!"

Peter followed Sarah toward the big gaping hole in the wall that led out to the lawn. They stood in front of it, waving their arms just as Alan and Judy had. The pelican headed for Sarah first, but at the last moment it veered off . . . straight toward Peter!

Peter had never seen a bird so big. Its wingspan must have been more than six feet! The giant pelican dove, its long, pointed beak aimed straight at Peter's head. Peter stood and waved. The pelican had turned away when the others did that. Why didn't it turn away now? It just kept coming, and coming . . .

16

At the last second, Peter ducked and covered his head. The pelican swooped past him, out the hole in the wall, and flapped away through the trees.

Giving Peter a disgusted, scornful look, Alan sprinted toward the hole. Peter winced with humiliation.

"I'm sorry," he tried to say. "That pelican scared me."

Alan ignored him and raced off after the bird. Sarah came up behind Peter and put her hand reassuringly on his shoulder.

"Don't let him get to you," she said softly. "He's the *last* person you want as a role model."

Judy joined them and pointed at Alan. "Where's he going?"

"Probably toward the water," Peter guessed. "That's what pelicans like, isn't it?"

"We better follow," Judy said. But the words were hardly out of her mouth when the muffled sound of a telephone ringing reached their ears.

Looking around the wreckage of the room, it was hard to believe that a telephone had survived without at least being knocked off the hook. Judy followed the ringing sound and found the phone under a pile of broken plaster. Peter stood nearby and listened as his sister answered.

"Hello? . . . Oh, hi, Aunt Nora . . . well, I can't really talk right now. . . . No, a stampede of wild animals just ran through the house. And a dozen monkeys destroyed the kitchen and there's this huge lion locked in your bedroom. Right . . . no, I understand . . . okay, 'bye."

With a frown, Judy hung up the phone and looked at her brother. "I just got grounded for another week."

Meanwhile, Sarah was gazing through the big hole in the living room wall. "This goes against my best instincts, kids," she said. "But I think we better go see what Alan's up to."

They headed out of the hole and through the woods toward the Brantford River. Soon they were tromping around trees and over twigs near the riverbank. Not far away they could hear the churning sound of rushing water.

"Alan?" Judy called out.

"Shhhhhhhhh!" came the reply.

Peter and the others stopped and looked around. Alan was crouched nearby behind the tall reeds, waving excitedly at them to get down. Everyone kneeled and watched as he crept through the reeds and bulrushes. Finally he parted some reeds and all of them could see the pelican perched on a big flat rock that stuck a few feet out into the river. The Jumanji game lay at its feet near the edge of the rock. It could fall into the river at any moment.

Peter saw the fix Alan was in. Not only did he have to try to get the board from the pelican, but he had to make sure the game didn't fall into the water. Alan started to crawl up on the rock. So far the pelican didn't see him.

Then suddenly the bird spun around and glared at him!

"Easy there, bud," Alan said, stretching his hand out toward the game. "You've got something of mine."

The pelican answered by jerking its beak forward and snapping at Alan's hand.

"*Yeow!*" Alan pulled his injured hand back and cradled it. Watching nearby, Peter, Judy, and Sarah winced at the imagined pain.

But Alan would not be deterred. Now he crawled over to another part of the rock that looked out over the water.

"Okay, let's try the barter system," he said. As Peter and the others watched, amazed, Alan stared down in the water, then thrust his hands in and came up with a large, flapping trout!

"Unreal!" Peter gasped.

Alan was instantly on his feet, dangling the fish in front of the bird, who hopped eagerly toward him.

"Oh, you like this, huh?" Alan tossed the fish toward another part of the rock. The pelican lurched forward, scooping it up with its beak. Meanwhile, Alan reached for the game board and . . . missed!

Splash! The board fell into the water and started to float downstream with the current. Peter charged out of the bushes and started to run toward the riverbank. Leaping over rocks and fallen trees, he headed downriver, hoping to intercept the game.

But the game was being swept out toward the middle. He'd never be able to get it!

Just then he spotted the trunk of a tree which had fallen and was jutting out over the river. Peter hesitated for a second, then jumped up on the trunk. He crawled out over the river, but the trunk was too high above the water for him to reach.

There was only one thing Peter could do. He crawled onto a branch about as wide as the thick part of a baseball bat. Even that was too high to reach the water, but if he hung upside down with his knees bent over the branch, his fingers almost reached the surface.

The Jumanji game was floating quickly toward him. Hanging upside down, Peter started to swing, making the branch creak and bounce. One . . . two . . . three! He bounced down, grabbed the box and swung back up!

A second later he was crawling back along the tree trunk to the shore with the box. Judy and Sarah waited at the base of the tree, watching him with excited, amazed looks on their faces.

"Peter, that was *so cool!*" Judy gushed.

"Very intense," Sarah added with a smile.

But as much as Peter enjoyed their praise, it was Alan he needed to hear from the most.

"Nice work," Alan said tersely, and started to turn away. "Now let's get a move on."

Peter felt his shoulders sag in disappointment. Alan didn't seem impressed at all.

From where they were, the fastest way home was over an iron bridge that crossed the river. Peter and the girls started across it with Alan stalking ahead.

Screech! Suddenly Officer Bentley's battered and dented police car skidded to a stop beside them. Alan started to run, but Officer Bentley jumped out and grabbed him.

"Wouldn't you know an all points bulletin to

pursue a stampede of wild animals would lead straight to *you*," Bentley grunted as he twisted Alan's arm behind his back.

"I don't know what you're talking about," Alan replied.

"Fine." Officer Bentley started to push him toward the patrol car. "I'm taking you in for questioning."

Alan dug his feet in and fought back. "I'm not going anywhere."

"Oh, really?" In a flash, Officer Bentley slapped a pair of handcuffs on him and started to *drag* him toward the car. Peter knew they had to stop him. Once Alan was gone, they'd *never* be able to finish the game.

"Wait a minute!" Sarah cried desperately. "Please . . . uh . . . don't take him away . . . he's . . ."

"Her fiancé," Judy finished the sentence for her.

Officer Bentley stopped and frowned. "I thought you said he was your uncle."

"He is," Judy said. "But he's the half-brother of my mother's sister from her father's first marriage."

For a moment everyone was confused. Then Peter decided to chime in with his own phony plea: "Please don't take our half-uncle. He's the only family we've got."

Something weird must've happened because all of a sudden Alan changed his mind and started bobbing and jerking around like some kind of crazy person as he tried to drag Officer Bentley toward the car.

"It's all right!" Alan cried. "I'll be back soon. Let's go, Carl."

He pulled Officer Bentley toward the patrol car, as if he couldn't wait to be taken down to police headquarters and questioned. Sarah was outraged.

"*You* were the one who said you'd never abandon your friends!" she screamed at him. "And now you're just leaving us holding the bag."

"A bag's going to be holding *me* if you don't let me get out of here," Alan yelled, frantically pulling on the handcuffs. "Van Pelt's got me in his sights. Carl! Come on!"

Everything was going crazy, and it was all because of the game. Suddenly Peter had a stroke of genius. He knew everything was supposed to go back to normal once the game was finished. So, what if he just finished the game by himself?

With everyone else still yelling at Alan, and Alan himself hopping around like he had ants in his pants, no one noticed when Peter went off to the side and opened the game board. His token was exactly twelve squares from the end. Peter took out the dice and carefully positioned them in his fingers so both showed 6. All he had to do was drop them carefully so that they fell straight down. Then it would look like he'd rolled a 12 and everything would go back to normal.

By now, Alan and Officer Bentley were in the patrol car and Officer Bentley was telling the rest of them to go home. Peter dropped the dice.

The next thing he knew, he couldn't move. It felt as if some kind of spell had come over him. Not only that, but instead of going forward, his token went back to the beginning of the game. A cold, tingling terror swept through him.

"Judy!" he cried.

Judy came over and saw that the board was open. "What's wrong? What happened?"

Peter explained that he'd tried to end the game himself, and now he couldn't move. New words began to float up into the crystal: "'A law of Jumanji having been broken, you will slip back even more than your token.'"

"You tried to *cheat?*" Sarah gasped as she joined them.

Once again Peter explained what he'd done. Meanwhile, he was feeling the strangest sensation. His whole body was tingling.

"*Peter!*" his sister suddenly gasped. "*Look at your hands!*"

Peter looked down at his hands. His eyes widened and his chest became so tight it was impossible to breathe. Thick dark fur was growing out of the backs of his hands!

17

They had to get Alan back from the police. Sarah said that in order to do that you had to post bail, and in order to do *that*, you had to have money. And since none of them had much money, they'd have to go to town to get some.

They got a ride to town in the back of a pick-up. Clutching the Jumanji game tightly, Peter still had that tingling sensation, and Judy and Sarah kept giving him nervous looks. Every time Peter looked down at his hands, they looked a little hairier. And it was getting hard to sit for some strange reason. It occurred to him that he might be turning into a monkey. After all, the board said he'd be going backwards . . . back to a primate?

They got into town . . . or what was left of it. Everything was out of control. Cars were parked helter skelter on the sidewalks. People and monkeys were running in and out of stores as if they were on some insane spree. A man with yellowed skin, sweat glistening on his face, lurched past them, and a motorcycle raced down the street with three monkeys on board.

Sarah led them to a bank ATM machine and slid in her card. She pressed a bunch of keys, but a slip of paper came out saying the machine was temporarily out of service.

"Darn," Sarah muttered, searching through her pocketbook and pulling out a leather checkbook. "Maybe we can bail him out with a check."

"*Ahhhh!*" Judy suddenly screamed.

Peter and Sarah spun around and found the hunter Van Pelt behind them. He was carrying some new kind of high-powered rifle with a long scope on it.

"I'll take that." Van Pelt yanked the Jumanji game out of Peter's furry hands and waved it at them. "You can tell that coward that if he treasures this toy, he can meet me at . . ."

Van Pelt's voice trailed off as he looked down at the game with a fascinated expression on his face. He'd just noticed the picture of the great white hunter on the board, and that it looked *exactly like him!*

"Help!" "Look out!" "Run!" Just then, a large crowd of panicked townsfolk raced down the sidewalk past them. Van Pelt looked up for a moment to see what was going on. That was all the time Peter needed. He quickly snatched the game from the hunter's hands and dashed away into the street.

Screeech! A car skidded to a stop, missing Peter by inches. A big, red-faced man pushed open the car door and jumped out as if he was going to start yelling.

Ruuuuuuummmmmbbbbllllllle! Suddenly the street began to quiver and shake. The red-faced man and Peter looked up and saw a huge stampede of animals bearing down on them. The rhinos were in the lead, followed by the elephants, zebras, and other jungle animals. The red-faced man turned and ran. Peter quickly dove into the car.

The next thing he knew, the animals stampeded *right over the car!* Peter ducked down and looked up in horror as the roof was crushed and the windows shattered, covering him with nuggets of shatter-proof glass. With every passing animal, the roof was crushed lower and lower. Peter ducked down as low as he could go and was surrounded by dust, hooves, and flying debris. The roof kept dipping until Peter was certain he would be squashed.

But the stampede passed, and Peter wasn't squashed. He was, however, trapped inside the crushed car. The rough, tanned hands of Van Pelt reached in. Peter thought the hunter wanted to save him, but instead, the hands went around the Jumanji game.

"Give me that, boy." Van Pelt yanked the board out of his hands and loped away down Main Street.

"Help!" Peter shouted. "Get me out of here!"

Judy and Sarah reached into the crushed car and managed to pull him out.

"We have to get that game back," Sarah said, and started after Van Pelt, who went down the street and into a large discount store called Sir Save-A-Lot. People were running in and coming out with chairs, TVs, and other items Peter doubted they'd paid for.

They ran in and looked down the long aisles for a sign of the great white hunter, but all they saw were people pulling things off the shelves.

"Look!" Judy suddenly gasped. Halfway down an aisle, the Jumanji board lay on a glass display case. There was no sign of Van Pelt.

"Wait here," Sarah said and hurried toward the display case. As she reached for the game, a large weathered hand came out from behind the case and closed tightly around her wrist. Van Pelt rose up from his hiding place.

"I might have known." Sarah tried to struggle out of his grasp, but he was too strong.

"When Alan hears that I've got you, he'll come," Van Pelt said with a confident smile. "And then I'll bag him."

"Great plan, genius," Sarah shot back. "But how is Alan supposed to find out you've got me?"

With his free hand, Van Pelt raised his new rifle.

Blam! Blam! Blam! He fired it into the ceiling. All around the store, people screamed and fled out the doors. Sarah started to struggle again. Now Van Pelt leveled the rifle at *her!*

"Don't move, woman!" he threatened loudly enough for everyone in the store to hear, "or I'll jolly well blow you to chips and snippets!" Then he gestured to the fleeing people. "Alan will hear of your predicament soon enough."

Meanwhile, Judy and Peter had quietly sneaked up to the display case. Judy gave Peter, who was now more monkey than human, a nod. Peter jumped up and bit Van Pelt on the knee with his long sharp monkey teeth. At the same moment, Judy popped up with the counter's laser price reading gun and flashed it into Van Pelt's eyes.

"*Yaaaaaa!*" The great white hunter let go of Sarah's wrist and howled as the laser gun temporarily blinded him.

Sarah grabbed the game and the three of them started to run.

Blam! Blam! Blam! A row of large purple Barney dolls above Peter burst apart as Van Pelt fired at them. Peter raced toward the exit doors . . .

But Van Pelt got there first. Peter skidded to a stop.

"Where is she, monkey boy?" he bellowed, aiming his rifle right at Peter. Peter swallowed and took a step back, but there was no way he could escape now.

18

"Uh, she's over there!" Peter pointed to the right. The second Van Pelt turned, Peter took off to the left. With the great white hunter blocking the exit doors, he'd have to find another way to get out.

A few moments later he found himself in the sporting goods area, creeping past aisles filled with baseball mitts, fishing rods, and exercise machines.

Blam! Blam! From another part of the store came the report of Van Pelt's rifle as he hunted Sarah and the Jumanji game. Peter looked around and spotted an aluminum canoe. Nearby in the diving section were a couple of scuba tanks.

An idea started to form in his head, but to make it work, he'd first have to find some rope and pay a visit to the aisle containing laundry soap.

Minutes later he was pouring liquid laundry

detergent over the floor in the sporting goods section when Judy rushed past, pushing a shopping cart with the Jumanji game in it.

"Psst!" Peter hissed at his sister and got her attention. He motioned her to join him. Judy skidded to a halt and stared uncertainly at him.

"Peter?" Her forehead furrowed.

"Yeah." Peter knew why she was frowning. He'd almost completely changed into a monkey by now. "It's me," he whispered.

Judy nodded. After all, how many talking monkeys were there? "What?"

Peter quickly told her his plan.

"Are you crazy?" Judy gasped.

"Got a better idea?"

Judy shook her head.

"Okay," Peter said. "Just go down to the end of the aisle where the exercise machines are. Wait there until Van Pelt comes by and sees you. As soon as he starts down the aisle toward you, hide."

Judy just looked at him with a strange expression on her face.

"What's wrong?" Peter asked.

"I can't believe I'm talking to a monkey," she said.

"I'm not a monkey," Peter insisted. "I'm your brother. Now hurry!"

Peter hid behind a large box of basketballs. No sooner did Judy go off than Van Pelt raced up, breathing hard, his face red with rage and frustration. Way down at the other end of the aisle, Judy stepped out and waved at him. "Yoo-hoo!"

"You're mine now," Van Pelt muttered with a vicious grin and started down the aisle after her.

But he hadn't gone far before his hunting boots hit the liquid detergent and he started to skid and dance wildly in an effort to stay upright. That was Peter's cue to jump up and begin stage two. He pushed the canoe into position. Strapped on the back were several scuba tanks. Tied across the bow was the longest canoe paddle he could find. Peter lined up the canoe, then lifted a hammer high in the air.

Clang! He hit the valves on the scuba tanks as hard as he could, knocking them off.

Phhoooooosssssshhh! The compressed air shot out of the tanks and the canoe rocketed over the slippery floor . . . straight for Van Pelt!

Clunk! Van Pelt tried to dodge out of the way, but the bow of the canoe went between his legs and the paddle hit his knees.

Thunk! Van Pelt fell headfirst into the canoe, which rocketed down the aisle and through a family of mannequins all dressed for a camping trip. The mannequins burst apart, and various arms, legs, and heads joined Van Pelt for the rest of the trip, which ended when the canoe went through the

101

door of a large tent. The tent bulged, ripped, and collapsed around him.

"Come on, let's go!" Sarah appeared near Peter and Judy and urged them toward the store exits.

Blam! They were halfway there when one last rifle shot rang out. Peter stopped and turned to see what Van Pelt had hit.

"Peter, look out!" Judy screamed.

Peter spun around, but couldn't see what he was supposed to look out for. Then everything went dark as he was buried beneath an avalanche of tires! Van Pelt had shot the lock off a huge tire rack above him!

Trapped under the tires, Peter could hear Judy and Sarah race back and start pulling away tires from the pile, trying to free him. Then everything went quiet.

"Stop your cringing." Van Pelt's deep voice broke the silence. "It's unsportsmanlike to shoot defenseless women."

"That is absolutely the sickest thing I have ever heard!" Sarah replied.

Through a crack in the pile of tires, Peter saw Van Pelt yank the Jumanji game out of Sarah's hands.

"He will come to me now," Van Pelt said in a very self-satisfied way.

CRASH! Hardly were the words out of his mouth when Officer Bentley's police cruiser came flying through the store's front windows with a tremendous, earsplitting crash. The large glass windows shattered, showering the long rows of cash registers with glass.

Slam! Bang! Boom! Racks of shelves started to explode, and merchandise flew in all directions as the police car plowed through aisle after aisle . . . heading straight for Peter, Judy, Sarah, and Van Pelt!

19

With one final crash, Officer Bentley's patrol car slammed into a floor-to-ceiling display of paint cans and came to a stop. The mountain of cans tumbled down over Van Pelt, burying the great white hunter.

Alan jumped out of the police cruiser. Seeing Sarah and Judy he gasped, "You're all right! Where's Peter?"

Judy told him. The next thing Peter knew, Alan was pulling away the last of the tires. He stared at him with a look of shock. Peter looked down at himself and understood why. He was now one hundred percent monkey.

Sarah and Judy quickly explained how Peter had tried to cheat to end the game, and the game had punished him by turning him into a monkey.

"Well, we've got the game," Alan said. "The best thing we can do is get back to the house and finish it."

"Why can't we finish it here?" Sarah asked.

"The mosquitos," Alan explained. "We can't let them get us."

Clank! Everyone turned to see Officer Bentley drag himself out of the remains of his police cruiser. His hand was cuffed to the car door, which had fallen off with the last crash. For a moment Bentley and Alan faced each other.

"Do you want me to help you?" Alan asked.

"No! Never!" Bentley gasped more in fear than anger. He started away down an aisle, dragging the door behind him.

"Where are you going?" Alan asked.

"The tool department, where else?" replied Bentley.

Alan turned to the others. "Okay, let's go."

As they started out of the store, Judy asked why Officer Bentley didn't want Alan's help. Alan told them how twenty-six years ago Carl Bentley had worked on the sole-stamping line at Parrish Shoes and how he'd invented the first air-cushioned, leather-sided, high-topped sneaker ever. Then Alan told them how Bentley had showed him the proto-type one day and how he had accidentally put it down on the sole-stamping conveyor belt, where it got caught in the machine and wrecked it, and how that got Bentley fired by Sam Parrish himself.

"How did he wind up being a policeman?" Judy asked.

"The town was going downhill and a bad element was moving in," Alan explained. "They expanded the police force and Carl got a job."

"And how did he wind up being handcuffed to his own police car?" Sarah asked.

Alan explained how he'd convinced Officer Bentley to undo the handcuffs around his wrists, and how Alan had instantly locked one cuff on Bentley and the other on the patrol car.

"Why?" Judy asked.

"I had to finish the game," Alan explained. "I couldn't let Carl get in the way. But then we heard on the police radio that Van Pelt was holding you hostage here so I got him in the patrol car and drove down here."

"How did you know to crash through the window and knock the paint cans on Van Pelt?" Judy asked.

"Well, to tell you the truth, I didn't," Alan answered sheepishly. "The car had no brakes."

By now, they were on Brantford Street, just a block from the Parrish House. The discomfort Peter had been feeling ever since he started to change into a monkey was now so bad that it made him whimper and walk funny.

Sarah gave him a sad look and then turned to Alan. "Talk to him, Alan."

Alan slowed down and walked beside him. "Well, Peter, you cheated and now you're going to have to face the consequences like a man."

The pain was almost too much for Peter. He stopped and let out a cry.

"Come on, chin up," Alan said, thinking the cause of Peter's unhappiness was that he'd been turned into a monkey. "Crying never did anybody any good. If you've got a problem, you've got to face it."

Peter just sobbed, not because he was a monkey, but because being a monkey *hurt!*

Meanwhile, Alan looked as if he'd just had a major realization. "You're right! I'm totally insensitive. Twenty-six years buried in the darkest, remotest jungle, and I *still* turned out just like my father!"

The next thing Peter knew, Alan got on his knees and hugged him. "I'm sorry, Peter. Really."

"It's not that," Peter managed to whimper.

Alan looked shocked. "Then what *is* it?"

Peter whispered something in his ear and pointed down at his pants. At the bottom of his pants leg, the furry tip of a tail poked out. Peter had finally figured out the source of all that pain. Alan nodded and went behind him.

Rippppp! At the sound of Peter's pants ripping, the girls turned around and scowled. A moment later Peter felt immense relief. He was finally out of pain. Alan had ripped a hole in the back of his pants, thus making room for his tail to stick out.

Alan put his hands on Peter's monkey shoulders and leveled his gaze at him. "Now don't worry, Peter. We'll get you turned back into you in no time flat. We're going right back in there, and sitting down. Together we're going to finish this game, no matter what."

Peter felt reassured. He followed the others onto the Parrish property, up the walk to the front door. Alan pushed the door open, but didn't go in. Instead, he and the others stood in the doorway and gasped.

"Oh, no!" Sarah let out a little wail. The inside of the house was filled with vines. They covered the walls and anything that touched them. The crystal chandelier in the foyer was covered. Through the green leaves the light created an eerie dappled effect on the floor.

"Maybe we should play somewhere else," Sarah said, backing out of the doorway.

Alan shook his head. "No, I've been dealing with this stuff all my life. It's the stuff *out there* that throws me."

At his insistence, they all gathered on the marble floor of the foyer and kneeled around the game board. Alan placed the dice in Sarah's hand. For the first time since their "reunion" she gazed back at him, not with animosity, but an electric longing.

"Ahem," Judy cleared her throat. "Sarah, if you roll a twelve, you'll win. The game will be over!"

Sarah closed her eyes and rolled the dice. It was . . . a five.

Everyone sighed in disappointment. On the board, Sarah's piece moved and new words floated up in the center crystal: "'Every month at the quarter moon, there is a monsoon in your lagoon.'"

Sarah looked up. "Monsoon? It's a good thing we're inside. Judy, quick. It's your turn."

Judy was just about to pick up the dice when lightning cracked overhead. They all looked up in amazement.

"Was it my imagination, or did that lightning happen inside?" Sarah asked with a defeated groan.

The words were hardly out of her mouth when a thick dark cloud formed just beneath the ceiling.

Rain started to fall.

Inside the house.

Lightning flashed and thunder rumbled. The rain turned into a torrent! In no time the floor was covered with water, rising around everyone's ankles. The Jumanji game started to float away, but Alan grabbed it. Now the water was at their knees and rising amazingly fast.

"What do we do now?" Sarah cried.

20

"Get to higher ground!" Alan shouted.

They fought their way through the waist-deep water toward the staircase to the second floor, but when they got there they could see torrents of water cascading down the stairs from above.

"We have to try to get up!" Alan cried, but each time he tried to climb the stairs he was knocked off his feet and swept back down by the rushing water. By now the water was up to their chests. Judy and Peter were treading water in order to stay afloat.

Alan stared up at the chandelier in the foyer as if getting an idea.

"Come on!" He started to swim toward it.

"*Alan!*" Sarah suddenly let out a scream of total terror. Alan, Peter, and Judy turned and saw the scaly green snouts and bulging eyes of two *huge* twenty-five-foot crocodiles paddling down the hallway toward them.

"*Swim!*" Alan cried.

Splashing and churning through the water wildly, the four started toward the chandelier. Meanwhile lightning continued to crash and thunder boomed throughout the house. Driving rain pelted them. Looking over his shoulder, Peter could see the crocodiles in hot pursuit!

Just then the long dining room table floated by. Alan pulled himself up onto it and then helped the others on. Peter looked back at the water rising toward the ceiling in the living room. The crocodiles were gone!

Sarah looked over the edge of the table, down into the water. Suddenly the water exploded in her face.

Snap! Huge crocodile jaws snapped shut, just barely missing her nose.

"*Ahhhhhh!*" Sarah let out a scream to wake the dead as the crocodiles circled the table, looking for the chance to attack.

"Climb!" Alan shouted, cupping his hands together so the others could use them as a step up. Clutching the Jumanji game, Judy climbed up into the chandelier, followed by Peter.

But there was no room in the chandelier for

Sarah and Alan. Meanwhile, the crocodiles circled the table, eyeing them hungrily and licking their chops.

Suddenly one of the crocs lurched up and climbed on the far end of the table! The end Sarah and Alan were on shot up like a teeter-totter and crashed into the chandelier.

The next thing Peter knew, he was thrown from the chandelier and into the water!

"Help!" he cried, flailing around in the water.

Meanwhile, the table was tilting so steeply that Sarah was starting to slide . . . right down toward the crocodile's gaping mouth!

Alan grabbed Peter by his tail and yanked him out of the water.

"Oh no!" Sarah screamed as her feet hit the tips of the crocodile's upper and lower jaws. The croc opened and closed his mouth, scissoring Sarah's legs open and shut as she stood precariously over it.

Splash! Alan dove past her into the water, pulling the crocodile away and wrestling it. Thrashing and writhing, they both disappeared below the churning surface. Hearing the commotion, the other crocodile turned and dove as well.

Now it was two huge, vicious twenty-five-foot crocodiles against one defenseless man.

"Alan!" Sarah screamed.

21

Suddenly, and for no apparent reason, the water level began to plummet. It was as if someone had pulled the plug out of a bathtub. Alan and the crocodiles began to swim against the current washing them away. From the chandelier, Peter stretched out his paw as far as he could to Alan, who grabbed it. But the current was so strong it began to pull Peter off the chandelier.

With pleading eyes, Peter reached out to Judy, who grabbed his hand. Now *she* started to get pulled into the water. Sarah grabbed Judy's hand and held tight while the crocodiles were swept away. Now Peter could see that the front door was missing. Someone must have opened it, allowing the water to escape.

Finally the last of the water drained away and

the table settled on the floor. Alan jumped up on it and helped Judy and Peter down from the chandelier. Then he helped Sarah down. She slid into his arms. Their faces were close as they looked into each other's eyes.

"You wrestled an alligator for me," Sarah said in a charged mixture of awe and appreciation.

Alan blinked, and then stepped back, as if the moment was too much for him. "Uh, it was a crocodile actually. Alligators don't have that fringe on their hind legs."

Sarah pursed her lips in disappointment.

"Come on," Alan said. "We better get upstairs."

He started up the stairs. Meanwhile, Sarah shook her head. Peter gave her a puzzled look.

"Fear of intimacy," Sarah muttered and started up the stairs.

They reached the second floor landing, but there were vines everywhere. One side of the hall was blocked by one of those giant man-eating pods. On the other side of the hall that lion scratched angrily at Aunt Nora's door, trying to get out.

Everyone looked around nervously.

"We better head upstairs," Alan said. "The attic's safer."

They climbed up the spiral staircase and into the attic. Alan wiped his hand over an old steamer trunk to clear off the dust, then put down the game. The others gathered around him and slumped down on old crates and boxes. They were exhausted. Alan looked around at their faces. No one even had the energy to speak. He picked up the dice as if he was about to roll.

"Uh-oh." He stopped. "Did I forget to collect two hundred dollars last time I passed Go?"

Alan laughed at his own joke, but Peter and the others just shook their heads and groaned, utterly unamused.

"Okay, okay," Alan grumbled. "There's no law that says you can't have a sense of humor."

He rolled the dice. His token slid forward automatically and new words floated up in the crystal: "'You better watch just where you stand. The floor is quicker than quicksand.'"

Plop! The crate Alan was sitting on instantly started to sink into the floor!

Sarah grabbed the dice and Peter got the board. They dove from their seats and tumbled away as the floor beneath Alan became a thick, rippling wood-grained ooze. It grew and grew until it was a pool of goo ten feet across with Alan in the center!

As the others watched in horror, Alan frantically clung to the steamer trunk until . . . *gulp!* . . . it sank beneath him. No matter how hard he struggled, it didn't stop the sticky ooze from dragging him down.

"Alan, don't struggle," Sarah cried.

"Help!" Alan screamed, struggling for all he was

worth. The stuff was up to his chest!

Judy raced off and came back with a music stand. Alan grabbed one end and she held the other and . . .

It came apart!

"Heeeellllllllppppp!" Alan screamed.

Peter spotted an old trombone and raced off to get it. He came back and held it out to Alan, who grabbed the slide and . . .

It came apart!

"Stop giving me things that come apart!" Alan screamed.

Sarah grabbed an old chair. Holding one leg, she held it out to Alan who grabbed the back and . . .

It came apart!

Alan groaned. He had now sunk up to his chin! Sarah slid down on her stomach and plunged her arms into the ooze in a futile attempt to reach him.

Peter could see it was hopeless. Nothing would prevent Alan from disappearing beneath the floor, and with him went any chance of ever finishing the game!

22

With everything looking totally hopeless, Judy tried one last thing. She grabbed the dice and rolled them, hoping to get the number that would bring her token to the end of the game. But instead of moving forward, her token moved *back* as the following words appeared in the crystal lens: "'There is one thing that you will learn. Sometimes you must go back a turn!'"

Having seen his sister's token slide back, Peter turned woefully toward Alan and Sarah just as something miraculous occurred—the pool of liquid floor turned solid again!

It looked exactly like the old attic floor had, except for one thing—Alan and Sarah were stuck in it!

Alan's head was tilted back so that only the

117

front part of his face was showing, as well as his two outstretched forearms. Sarah was on her knees with her hands stuck in the wood. Once again their faces were only inches apart.

Peter and Judy quickly kneeled down around Alan's face.

"Thank you, Judy," Alan said, wincing. "That was quick thinking. Sarah and I would like to get out of the floor now. I believe it's Peter's turn."

Peter and Judy hurried back to the board. Meanwhile, Alan and Sarah's faces were so close again that they were almost kissing. Sarah giggled nervously.

"In my support group they'd say we were violating each other's personal space," she said.

"Is that bad?" Alan asked.

"Oh, yeah, it's a cardinal sin." Sarah grinned. "But I'm kind of enjoying it, really."

"Me, too," admitted Alan.

Meanwhile Peter picked up the dice and rolled. His token slid to a new spot and new words appeared: "'Need a hand? Why you just wait. We'll help you out, we each have eight.'"

The sound of hundreds of scuttling feet filled the attic. Then a spider the size of a cat dropped by a thread from a beam in the attic ceiling!

"*AAAAAHHHHHH!*" Judy and Sarah howled in unison. Peter spun around and looked into the dark corners of the attic where glistening red eyes had started to appear and emerge into the light. Giant spiders! Dozens of them!

With her hands still trapped in the attic floor, Sarah was quivering, paralyzed with fear. Judy quickly grabbed the top of the music stand and batted the closest spiders away.

"Peter!" Alan shouted. "My dad kept an ax in the woodshed! Get it!"

Peter scampered out of the attic and down the stairs past the creeping vines and locked-up lion. As he raced out the back door he heard someone scream. It was a different scream from Sarah's and Judy's, but he didn't have time to think about it. He ran across the backyard and up to the woodshed and grabbed the door.

But it wouldn't open!

Looking up, Peter saw the reason why. The doors were padlocked. Panicked, he looked around for something to break the door down. There! A rusty ax was leaning against the side of the shed. Peter grabbed it.

Wham! He slammed the ax against the padlock.

Wham! He *had* to get into the shed!

Wham! He had to get the . . .

Peter stopped and looked down at what was in his hands—an ax!

Idiot! Peter raced back toward the house with

the ax. He went in the back door and started to climb up the stairs. As he got to the second floor he came face to face with . . . Aunt Nora!

He *knew* he'd heard an unfamiliar scream before. Aunt Nora was staring at him with her mouth agape, as if she wanted to scream but couldn't.

"Aunt Nora!" Peter gasped. He was out of breath and scared silly, and his voice sounded like a screech. "It's me! Peter!"

"*Ahhhhhhhhhhhhh!*" Nora let out a scream that could have shattered glass, and stumbled backwards into the linen closet. Peter dashed forward and locked the linen closet door. At least she'd be safe from giant pods, mosquitos, and spiders!

"Can't talk now!" he yelled through the door. "Explain later!"

Up in the attic, Judy was batting away spiders with the music stand while Sarah and Alan watched helplessly. Suddenly Alan had an idea.

"Sarah!" he shouted. "It's your turn! All you need is a seven!"

"What am I supposed to do?" Sarah yelled back. "I can't roll!"

"Wait!" Alan cried. "Maybe you can!"

Alan bared his teeth at her. Suddenly, Sarah understood!

"Judy!" Alan yelled. "Bring the game, quick!"

As Peter entered the attic, Judy swatted away one last large spider and picked up the game. From under it rose up a poisonous purple flower, arching like a cobra, its poison barbs quivering.

"Judy!" Peter cried. "Look out!"

23

Too late! The vine lunged and its barbs struck Judy in the neck.

Wham! Peter swung the ax down, cutting the deadly flower in two.

"Judy, you okay?" Peter gasped.

"I'm fine," Judy answered, quickly brushing the barbs from her neck. "Help *them!*" Still carrying the game, she hurried over to Sarah.

"Give me the dice," Sarah said. "In my mouth."

Judy held out the dice and Sarah took them in her mouth and dropped them on the board. Her token started to move and another rhyme appeared in the crystal: "'You're almost there, with much at stake. But now the ground begins to quake.'"

Judy let out a scream and jumped back as another spider swung down right in front of her face. Peter swung the ax, lopping off the spider's thread. The spider hit the floor and headed toward him, but Peter belted it away with the ax.

"Oh no!" Judy let out a new scream. Peter wheeled around and found himself facing dozens more spiders. More than he could ever hope to fight off.

Everything looked hopeless!

But just then the spiders froze. A split second later they were scurrying madly toward the far corners of the attic.

"All right!" Peter shouted triumphantly and raised a furry clenched paw in the air.

"Wait a minute," Alan cautioned. "Listen."

Peter stood still. For a second there was no sound or movement around him. Then the walls began to rattle.

Thunk! Next to him Judy suddenly collapsed on the floor. Peter bent down. His sister looked pale, and a fine perspiration had broken out along her brow. Peter sat down and gently placed her head in his furry lap.

"Oh, no!" he cried in despair.

"What's wrong?" Sarah asked.

"She was stung by one of the purple flowers," Peter said. "What's going to happen to her?"

"We've got to end the game," Alan said. Then to Sarah he quietly added, "It's her only chance."

The floor began to shake violently and the

unmistakably loud rumble of an earthquake filled the air. Old armoires fell over and stacks of dusty magazines spilled to the floor. Peter cradled his sister's head in his arms.

"You're going to be okay," he said softly. "Does it hurt?"

"No," she answered with a grimace.

"Liar," Peter said, but with affection.

Judy moaned. "I wish Mom and Dad were here."

Crack! The attic floorboards began to crack and separate. A fissure appeared at one end of the attic. Floorboards splintered, plastic fell, pipes and wires snapped and sparked! The ground under the house was splitting. The house was beginning to pull apart!

As the floor came apart, Sarah was able to pull her hands free. The boards around Alan's face fell away, leaving nothing to hold him up. Suddenly he was hanging above a deep bottomless chasm!

24

"Alan!" Sarah dived forward and grabbed his arms. Now she was lying on the floor, holding him while he hung over the ever-widening chasm!

A foot away the Jumanji game teetered on the splintered edge of some boards.

"Grab the game!" Alan yelled.

"I won't let you go!" Sarah yelled back.

Alan pulled one hand free and grabbed for the game but missed! The game fell through the sections of the house, landing on a broken floorboard far below. Beneath that floorboard was nothing but an empty, dark, bottomless abyss.

Alan had one chance left. He broke free from Sarah, grabbed onto a nearby vine, and swung like Tarzan through the house. At the end of the first arc, he gracefully switched in midair to another vine, swinging down into the chasm and grabbing the game before it disappeared forever!

He swung up out of the chasm and let go, landing in the middle of the living room. Alan was panting for breath and near exhaustion. Wiping a cold sweat from his eyes, he set the game on the floor and pulled the dice from his pocket. This was the moment he'd been waiting twenty-six years for. It was hard to believe that it was finally here. He kneeled down and picked up the dice.

"I'm going to do it!" he said to himself. "I'm going to end this game once and for all!" He raised his hand to throw the dice.

"*Don't move!*" a voice ordered from behind him.

Alan felt a chill run up his spine and he slowly turned and looked over his shoulder at Van Pelt, who had his rifle trained on him. The great white hunter wasn't actually white anymore. Ever since his collision with the paint display at the Sir Save-A-Lot, he was more like the great multicolored hunter.

"Shouldn't you be running?" Van Pelt asked, puzzled by Alan's reaction.

"Not right now," Alan replied, turning back to the board, which Van Pelt could not see. "I've got more important things to do."

Van Pelt kept the rifle trained on the back of Alan's head. "Is this some kind of trick?" he asked suspiciously. "What's that in your hand?"

"Nothing," Alan replied.

"Nothing?" Van Pelt's eyes narrowed. "Then drop it."

"You better do what he says," Sarah said, entering the room from the remains of the broken second floor staircase.

Alan let go of the dice. One fell on the game board and rolled a 3. The other hit the edge of the board, bounced off, tumbled across the floor, and disappeared out of sight into the earthquake crevice!

Alan and Sarah stared after it, wide-eyed. Without the dice, they'd *never* be able to finish the game!

"You call that better things to do?" Van Pelt asked contemptuously. "Like play with toys? Playtime is over, little boy. You better run."

But Alan shook his head. He was tired of running. He was tired of being in this game. If it wasn't going to end this way, he was willing to take another way out.

"But you *have* to run," Van Pelt said, looking exasperated and confused. "I'll even let you run until I count three. One . . ."

Alan stood before him and didn't budge.

"Two," Van Pelt growled, staring down the barrel at him.

Alan stared back.

"*Three!*" Van Pelt said.

Alan held his ground. Instead of firing, Van Pelt lowered the rifle and nodded.

"At last you have proven yourself," the great multicolored hunter said.

Alan smiled proudly. But his smile faded as Van Pelt again raised the rifle and aimed it at him.

"You are worthy quarry," Van Pelt said, starting to squeeze the trigger. "Any last words?"

Alan's eyes darted around. Suddenly he looked down at the Jumanji board. To his amazement, his token had moved to the finish! He could feel his eyes bug out.

"Uh, Jumanji?" Alan swallowed hoarsely.

Blam! Van Pelt fired!

25

"NNNNNNNOOOOOOOO!" Sarah screamed and threw herself in front of Alan.

But the bullet never hit her. A strong wind whipped up out of nowhere, whooshing around the walls of the living room. Sensing the game was ending, Alan and Sarah fell into each other's arms and held tight, their eyes squeezed closed.

Van Pelt turned into a wisp of smoke and vanished. The swirling wind grew stronger, whipping around the house like a tornado with Sarah and Alan at the center. Suddenly the walls exploded, and everything from the world of Jumanji—the vines, giant mosquitos, spiders, monkeys, rhinos, elephants, zebras, and more—whirled in tighter and tighter until . . .

Shhhuuummmppp! They were all sucked back into the center of the game board.

Everything became quiet.

Alan slowly let go of Sarah and opened his eyes. Something had changed. He looked into her face and she into his. She looked . . . like the girl he'd known when he was twelve. Was it possible?

Sarah's thirteen-year-old mouth opened in astonishment as she and Alan recoiled from each other in shock. It was 1969 again! They were kids again!

They heard the front door in the foyer open. Sam Parrish strode in, his face as red and angry as the last time Alan had seen him twenty-six years before. Alan felt a lump in his throat. His father was alive again!

"Dad," he stammered. "You're *back*."

"I forgot my speech notes," Sam replied stiffly.

Alan dashed across the room and threw his arms around his father. His father froze. He'd never seen such a display of emotion from his son before.

"Dad, Dad!" Alan gasped happily. "I'm so glad you're back!"

"I've only been gone five minutes," Sam said, puzzled.

"It seems like a lot longer to me," Alan replied.

Sam Parrish laughed uncertainly. Feeling his son's arms around him must have felt so good that he dropped his usual reserve and hugged him back.

"Hey, I thought you weren't ever talking to me again," Sam said.

"Whatever I said, I'm sorry," Alan apologized, and *really* meant it.

Sam gazed down at his son for a long silent moment. "Look, Alan, I was angry. I'm . . . sorry too. And about Cliffside Academy . . ."

"Cliffside?" The name sounded vaguely familiar, but at that moment Alan couldn't remember why.

"Right." His father nodded. "Why don't we talk it over tomorrow, man-to-man?"

Having just recently been a thirty-eight-year-old man, Alan didn't want to be reminded. "How about father-to-son?" he asked.

"Sure." Sam Parrish backed away and blinked. "Hey, I've got to get going. I'm the guest of honor."

He turned away.

"Uh, Dad?" Alan said.

Sam stopped.

"Back in nineteen sixty . . . er, I mean . . . you know *today* that machine in the factory that broke? It wasn't Carl Bentley's fault. I accidentally put that shoe on the assembly line."

He and his father exchanged a long look. It seemed to Alan that his father was finally seeing him in a new light.

"I'm glad you told me, son," Sam said. Then he turned and left.

Alan turned to Sarah and smiled. His eyes went to the game board and the smile disappeared. "Judy and Peter!" he gasped. "We gotta get up to the attic!"

He spun around, but Sarah grabbed his arm to stop him. "They're not there, Alan. We're back in nineteen-sixty-nine. They don't even *exist* yet."

She held out her hand and opened it, revealing Peter's and Judy's tokens. Alan looked down at them and nodded sadly. She was right.

"We're back," Sarah said. "Everything's the same as it used to be."

"Except for one thing," Alan said, turning and heading for the kitchen.

"Where are you going?" Sarah asked.

"To get something." Alan disappeared and came back a moment later with a paper shopping bag. He put the Jumanji game in it and led Sarah outside.

A little while later, they were riding double on his new English racer. Sarah held the shopping bag in her lap. Alan rode to the bridge over the Brantford River and stopped in the middle. Sarah got off and opened the bag. Alan reached in and took out the Jumanji game, which now had two heavy rocks tied to it.

Ker-splash! Alan heaved the game over the

bridge railing and watched it plunge into the turbulent river below. He and Sarah watched as it disappeared in the churning waves.

Even after the game was gone, they stood at the railing, staring down at the river.

"I'm starting to forget what it's like to be a grown-up," Sarah said.

"Me too," said Alan. "That's okay, as long as we don't forget each other."

"Or Peter and Judy," Sarah said.

They looked into each other's eyes.

"There's something I've really been wanting to do," Sarah said. "I think I better do it before I feel *too* much like a kid."

She stepped close and gave him a long kiss on the lips. When it was over, they smiled at each other and walked back to Alan's bike, holding hands.

26

It was a cold winter's day. Chunks of ice floated down the Brantford river and icicles hung from the windows of the Parrish Shoe Company where the big sign now read:

PARRISH SHOES—FIVE GENERATIONS OF QUALITY

Alan Parish, thirty-eight, walked along the hallway outside the executive offices. The walls were covered with red and green Christmas decorations and a Christmas tree festooned with candy canes stood at the end of the hall. Alan's hair was neatly trimmed, his tie was tucked in, and his shirtsleeves rolled up. A shorter man wearing a rumpled suit and carrying several thick ledgers under his arm walked alongside him. His name was Marty, and he was the company accountant.

"The retailers are furious that you're planning to give away all those shoes again this Christmas," he was saying.

"The kids I'm giving these shoes to aren't going to go out and buy ninety-dollar sneakers," Alan replied with a smile. "It's not like anyone's going to lose business."

"Except *us*." Marty shook his head wearily.

"Look at it like this," Alan said. "When these kids grow up and get jobs, they'll remember Parrish Shoes and become loyal customers."

As they passed another office, Carl Bentley, now forty-five, stepped out wearing a dark suit and tie.

"It's an investment in our future," he said, as if completing Alan's thought. He put his arm around Marty's shoulder and gave Alan a wink that the accountant couldn't see. "Come on into my office, Marty. Why don't you and I work out the details?"

Marty nodded, knowing he couldn't win. He followed Carl into the office and shut the door. On the outside of the door were the words:

CARL BENTLEY—PRESIDENT

That night Alan, dressed in a Santa suit and wearing a long white beard, stood in the kitchen of the Parrish house, talking to his father on the phone. A few years back, Sam Parrish and his wife had retired from the shoe business and moved to Florida.

"The hiking boot line's been doing great," Alan was saying. "Yeah, it's been another terrific year."

All around him the kitchen counters were covered with platters of food. The kitchen door swung open and Sarah, her face flushed and radiant, waved at him.

"They're here, hon," she whispered.

Alan nodded. "Dad, I've gotta run. My new marketing director just showed up. Give Mom my love and we'll see you in a couple of days."

Alan hung up and made his way into the foyer, carrying two shoe boxes wrapped in gift paper. The room was crowded with people who'd come for the party. A dozen kids ran around, plucking candy canes from trees and chasing each other. Sarah was standing with a nicely dressed man in his mid-thirties and his pretty wife.

"Jim, glad you could make it!" Alan gave the man's hand a vigorous shake.

"Thanks," Jim Sheperd said. "This is my wife, Martha."

Alan said hello. Meanwhile, Jim looked around at the crowd.

"Where are the kids?" he asked his wife.

A twelve-year-old girl and eight-year-old boy

were pushing their way through the crowd. Alan felt a moment of shock, then forced himself to recover.

"Here are your kids," he said.

"How did you know?" Martha looked puzzled.

"Just a guess," Sarah replied, giving Alan a wink.

"Well, you're right," Jim said. "This is Judy and Peter. Kids, meet Mr. and Mrs. Parrish."

"Hi." Peter shook Alan's hand.

"Nice to meet you," said Judy. Neither showed any recognition of Alan or Sarah.

"We feel like we already know you," Sarah said.

"Because we've heard so much about you," Alan added hastily.

He gave the shoe boxes to Peter and Judy. "Merry Christmas, kids."

The kids started to unwrap the boxes. Alan and Sarah watched, utterly absorbed in the happiness of seeing them again. Then Alan snapped out of it.

"So, when can you start work?" he asked Jim.

"Well, actually, Martha and I were thinking about taking a little skiing trip up in the Canadian Rockies," Jim said. "Sort of a second honeymoo—"

"No!" Alan and Sarah both gasped at the same time. The outburst was so unexpected that for a moment the entire room went silent.

Alan looked around at the startled faces and felt his own face turn flushed and red. He turned back to Jim. "Uh, sorry, it's just that we—"

"Really need to get the campaign for the new line going." Sarah finished the sentence for him.

Jim glanced at his wife and nodded. "No problem. We can always take the trip another time. Maybe we'll wait until the summer and go to the Cape instead. In the meantime, I can start next week."

Alan breathed a sigh of relief. By now, Peter and Judy had torn open the shoe boxes and each pulled out a brand-new pair of sneakers.

"Cool shoes!" Peter gasped.

Judy read the name on them. "Jumanjis!"

"What do you think?" Alan asked.

"Great sneakers, weird name," Peter said with a shrug.

Alan and Sarah just looked at each other and smiled.

EPILOGUE

That summer, two young French girls strolled along the beach near Nice, France.

"My mother and father are always criticizing me," one said to the other. "They never let me have any fun."

"It's the same at my house," replied the other. "Nobody appreciates me."

A little ways away, half buried in the wet sand at the water's edge, was a strange-looking wooden box.

Brummm-tum-tum! Brummm-tum-tum! came a peculiar drumming sound from within.